Books by Jeffrey Kelly

Tramp Steamer and The Silver Bullet
The Basement Baseball Club

The Basement
Baseball Club

The Basement Baseball Club

Jeffrey Kelly

Houghton Mifflin Company
Boston

Library of Congress Cataloging-in-Publication Data

Kelly, Jeffrey, 1946–
   The basement baseball club.

   Summary: The Roader team members spend the summer
trying to beat their local rivals in sandlot baseball.
   [1. Baseball—Fiction]   I. Title.
PZ7.K2962Bas   1987   [Fic]   86–27545
ISBN 0-395-40774-5

Printed in the United States of America
VB 10 9 8 7 6 5 4

to sandlot baseball players everywhere

Contents

The Basement
Baseball Club

1
Nicknames and a Problem

"Fungofandanglefat!"

"What in blazes is the matter now, Keyboard?" I called out from across the room. Keyboard was the nickname for Jack Kunkle Smith, who was, among other things, an aspiring pianist. At least he was according to his mother. Keyboard was also the most foul-mouthed kid I'd ever known. When he swore, which was often, the words all ran together like he had a mouth full of mothballs and came out a high-pitched squeal. Think of a broken water faucet. "Fungofandanglefat!" or "Zapashucamarmalade!" or a shortened "Twirpitch!" It was only by listening very closely that you could pick out the words, all of them dirty.

"I can't get the twirpitch tenpin to go down," he said morosely, overly dramatic as usual. He could've been on-stage.

Keyboard, Wart Embry — all two hundred pounds of him — and Leroy "Slam" Sanders were bowling down in my basement, the three of them hovering around one end of a long, narrow sheet of shiny cardboard, which served as a miniature bowling lane. At the opposite end a single white-and-blue-striped bowling pin, about half regulation size, was wobbling in place. The rest of the plastic pins were scattered all over the concrete floor.

"Be there!" Keyboard chortled, aiming for a spare. The tenpin went sailing one way, the ball he'd fired the other. Wart and Slam looked at each other disgustedly. Keyboard, a fierce competitor, was tough to beat.

My basement was the perfect place for a clubhouse. Warmed by the furnace in the winter, cool and damp in the summer, it had its own back-door entrance and was filled with every kind of game and sports equipment you could think of. There were even a couple of lumpy couches my mother'd found discarded by the side of the road, a Styrofoam ice chest, a makeshift table, and four or five weirdly shaped chairs. Right now it was a big pile of junk from one end to the other, but that's how we liked it. And since my parents didn't seem to mind (my mother screamed about it only once in a while), we kept it that way — cluttered and fun.

My best friend, Albert D., AD for short, and I were locked in a friendly game of Parcheesi. AD would've rather been playing something else, something that required more brain power, such as chess or Scrabble, but I wanted to focus most of my attention on the radio, which at that moment was broadcasting the White Sox game. An electrical storm had filled the airwaves with static, though nearby Chicago, where the game was being played, didn't seem to be affected. The Sox ground crew had managed to stay off the field; meanwhile, the announcer sounded as if he were talking into the microphone from a rocking chair, his voice drifting in and out, getting louder and softer, sometimes inaudible, with an occasional shout of excitement. "HOME . . . run!"

"Who homered?" Slam asked. He was getting set to take aim at the bowling pins, now reset at the end of the lane.

"A Soxer, I think," I told him, my ear to the radio.

"You wish," said AD. He fingered his eyeglasses, pushing them back on his nose, which had a Band-Aid on it from where he'd smashed into a tree chasing a long fly ball. A week ago the nose had been red and swollen to twice its size. Keyboard kept calling him "AD Adenoids" until AD had asked him to stop. AD could get anybody to do anything.

"Your move," he said to me.

He meant my turn. I picked up the dice and fired double sixes. "Take that!" I shouted at him.

CRASH! Bowling pins scattered across the floor.

"Fungofandanglefat!"

"A pack of gum says you can't name five former major leaguers with animal nicknames," AD said. He loved challenging the rest of us. A standout center fielder and the McCarthy Roaders' number two hitter, AD was also our resident major league baseball statistical expert. He knew just about all there was to know about the sport. I had the feeling that he'd practically memorized the entire *Baseball Encyclopedia*.

"Never mind that now," I said to him. "What about this Saturday? How're we gonna beat the Poisons?" The Hemlock Street Poisons were our hated baseball rival.

"We're p-probably n-not," said Wart. The words came out of his mouth like water through a clogged drainpipe. He was stooped over, resetting the striped bowling pins. Everything Wart did, including speaking and catching (he was our catcher) was in slow motion. He had an incredibly wide, beehive-shaped body. At the Aquacenter, the town pool, he kept his shirt on the whole time, even swimming. He said it was because he was allergic to the sun, but I knew better. He was embarrassed about being so fat and didn't know what else to do about it. Even so, he took a lot of razzing.

My own body, size small, resembled a pint-size jar of calamine lotion, the junk you spread all over yourself when you get poison ivy.

"The heck with you," Keyboard said to Wart. "That's loser talk. If you feel that way, don't play." He meant it.

"I-I only m-meant —" Wart began, but Keyboard cut him off.

"WHOOP-DE!" he hollered, chucking the bowling ball he was holding at the ceiling. Keyboard hated to lose, and we'd lost an unbelievable eight straight games to the Poisons.

"We'll kill 'em this time," Keyboard said. "If everybody tries."

"Right," I said.

"Yeah," said AD sarcastically. "And if Games pitches a no-hitter."

I looked over at Slam, who, even though he hadn't said anything, looked as worried as the rest of us.

"Fffft . . ." the radio crackled, ". . . ground ball to short." Outside there was a loud clap of thunder.

The problem with the Poisons was this. For years, as long as I'd been playing, the rivalry with them had been close, the two teams, Poisons and Roaders, splitting wins and losses. Kids came and went, moved in and out of the neighborhood, though most of the teams' players stayed pretty much the same. Often the games were decided by one run: good, close competition. Then last summer Bull Reilly arrived and everything changed. Bull could throw a fast ball through a concrete wall. No way we could hit it. The Poisons had won eight straight games, including three this year, games that weren't even close. Some of their players had begun to grumble that they should start looking around for better competition. More than anything, even a new ten speed bike, I wanted to see them eat their words. The only way to do that was to beat them on the field. The question was how.

"Hey, what gives?"

The voice on the stairs, like a cat crying, belonged to PJ "Games" Murphy, our southpaw pitcher. Games's real name was Paul James, but his nickname suited him better. In trouble more than out (the police knew him by sight), he never failed to miss practice, yet somehow always managed to show up for the games. And so —

Games. Keyboard, I guess because of the police, sometimes called him Chains.

Games — or Chains — slammed the back door at the top of the stairs and came on down. He was out of breath from running. The rain outside had plastered down his hair, which took on all the characteristics of a fetid swamp: yellow, oily, and smelly. When it was dry, Games's hair ballooned out and frizzed, like yellow cotton candy.

"The new people've . . . moved in," he said excitedly, taking a deep breath and pushing wet strands of hair out of his eyes and mouth. "The moving van's here . . . an' everything."

"Among the movers," AD asked, "are there any ballplayers?"

The radio crackled, but we'd stopped listening. All eyes were on Games. Another ballplayer or two for the Roaders was something we'd all talked about.

"I did see two kids," he said. "A girl, skinny as a straw. An' . . ." He gave his head a quick shake. Water sprayed out all over, splattering me, the closest. I started to complain but Keyboard stopped me. "Out with it, Chains!" he demanded.

Games was smiling, a grin like a slash across his face.

"Like I said, a girl, an' a kid our age, maybe older. Big like you wouldn't believe. An' strong. I saw him lift one end of a couch the size of a pickup truck. All by himself."

"Big as Bull Reilly?" Slam asked.

Games hesitated a moment. "As tall," he said at last.

"But skinny, like his sister. Strong looking." This last part he said with certainty.

"You talk to him?"

"No. I thought we could all go over together."

"What're we waiting for?" I shut off the radio with a bang. Sox game or not, Games's news was of major importance. Keyboard threw the bowling ball across the room and the six of us, with mounting excitement — we needed another good ballplayer something awful — headed up the stairs.

2
The First Sign
of Trouble

The six of us gathered beneath the roof of the carport outside my back door and waited for the rain to let up. The rain hitting the roof sounded like kernels popping in a popcorn popper. Partway down the street, on the same side, a whale of a moving van was parked in front of a brick two-family house that'd been empty since spring. A floor-to-roof door had been opened in the middle of the van and a ramp lowered onto the front lawn, the grass more brown than green. A couple of moving men stood at the top of the ramp inside the truck, doing what we were doing — keeping dry. The new kid was nowhere to be seen.

And then there he was, coming out the front door with his sister.

"Let's get a move on," I suggested.

We closed in on them in a hurry, AD, the fastest, up ahead, the rest of us close behind. Even Wart, who liked rain almost as much as a giant-size glass of prune juice and who ran about as fast as a tree, was doing his best to keep up. All told, the run from the carport to

the new kid's front porch took about twenty seconds
— just long enough to get soaked.

The new kid and his sister heard us coming, what
with our feet pounding on the pavement and Keyboard
whooping up his usual fuss. "Zapashucamarmalade!"
They stood together, leaning against the porch railing,
the kid looking uncomfortable, as if he had his pants
on too tight, his sister scared, like she was about to get
run over by a twelve-wheeler.

"Name's Shooter Carroll," I said, all business.
(Shooter: marbles, not basketball.) "What's yours?"

The kid was big — Games was right — with a flat,
pancake face and a pointy nose the color of a strawberry,
same color as the hair on his head. His shoulders stuck
straight out like a couple of two-by-fours. His arms,
elongated like the rest of him, looked powerful enough
to drive home runs over Gertie Gershwin's left field
roof, no sweat. He stared down at me, at all of us, before he answered.

"John Johnson," he said in a voice a whole lot deeper
than mine. "And," he looked at his sister, "that's Olive."

Olive? What a name! I heard a few snickers behind
me.

"Where're you from?" I asked him.

"New York." He took a step backward and stuck his
hands halfway in his pockets with his thumbs sticking
out. Olive sat down on the railing. She had a face like a
vanilla cupcake, flat and white with a strawberry stuck
in the middle. She looked about ten, maybe eleven, but
at that moment I wasn't too interested. That would
change, in a lot of ways.

"New York City!" I said excitedly. "Are you a Yankees fan? Mets?"

"Upstate New York," the kid said. "Mets."

"I'm a Yankees fan," Olive squeaked. "And White Sox."

I began to suspect there was something special about her.

"What position do you play?" I asked the kid.

"Play?" he said. He took another step backward, bumping into some cartons, his eyes shifting nervously. He wiped his mouth with the back of his hand. Olive shifted uneasily in her seat. Behind me there was a lot of shuffling. Someone coughed, AD I think. The movers, carrying a bulky piece of furniture covered by a burlap sack, probably as protection against the rain, came grunting and straining up the ramp. They smelled bad.

"Yeah, play," Keyboard said, speaking up for the first time. "Play. As in baseball."

"We need a good right-handed pitcher," Slam added, nudging my shoulder. "Or a good stick who can play the field."

"A veritable superstar," said AD.

We all laughed. Olive sort of smiled. The kid just stood there looking uncomfortable.

"Olive plays," he said.

"Shortstop," she said, again a squeak.

"We already have a shortstop," I said. "Me."

"Olive can play anywhere," said the kid. "She can hit, too."

I was beginning to get the idea that there was something wrong.

"What do you play?" I asked him again.

"I don't," the kid said.

None of us said anything. The rain sounded loud on the roof. The movers, having squeezed the piece of furniture through the front door, came out again and lumbered down the ramp.

"Whaddaya mean you don't play?" I found it impossible to believe a kid as big and strong as this one wouldn't like sports, especially baseball. Impossible. But before the kid could answer, Games spoke up.

"Wait a minute," he said, his voice high and scratchy. You could tell he was excited. "I know you. We were at a baseball camp together a few years ago, before my family moved to Chicago. John Johnson, that's right. You were the best baseball player at camp. Once for fun you hit a baseball clear across the lake. That was you, wasn't it?"

The rest of us turned from Games to the new kid, but he just shrugged. Then he smiled out of the corner of his mouth, wrinkling one side of his face and closing one eye. His eyebrows twitched nervously.

"I don't play anymore," he said.

"But you still like baseball?" I asked.

The kid nodded.

"Then why —"

"He just doesn't play," said Olive. "Not anymore."

We all looked at her, as puzzled as could be, then back at the kid.

"It's none of your business," he said. The look on his face, the half smile that had become a frown, made me swallow — hard.

"We sure could use another good player," I said truthfully.

"You've got one," the kid said. "Olive."

Olive.

"Okay," I said to her. "Practice tomorrow, out back, ten A.M. We've got a big game to get ready for on Saturday. See you then, er, Olive. Bring your glove. You, too," I said to the kid, "if you change your mind."

"He won't," said Olive.

Weird.

3
The Cartwheel Queen

Don't get me wrong. It's not that a kid, any kid, had to play baseball to get along with the McCarthy Roaders. He didn't. There were plenty of kids in the neighborhood, right there on the same street, who didn't care a hoot about our sandlot games against Bull Reilly and the rest of the muscle-head Hemlock Street Poisons, or the won-loss record of the beloved White Sox, or AD's baseball quizzes, or . . . well, anything that had to do with the sport. We all knew kids who didn't know an RBI from an ERA, Comiskey Park from Wrigley Field, Texas leaguers from infield pops. Kids who couldn't care less. Kids who would no more sit down with you to a game of dice baseball than stick their heads in a bucket of rosin. They liked competing, some of these kids. They were good in school, or, like Keyboard, could play a musical instrument, put a car's engine together blindfolded, race ten-speeders, whip you at any board game you could think of. They just didn't like baseball. Which was fine with me; except during the season who wanted to spend any time with them? Not the Basement Baseball Club, as we liked to call ourselves. We were kids who lived for baseball.

Games told us all about John Johnson. The camp was in upstate New York, where Games used to live. Games was younger than Johnson and played with the "Minis," while Johnson and the older kids played with the "Baddies" or "Maddies," Games couldn't remember which. Johnson, he told us with certainty, was the star. He could pitch "as fast as Bull Reilly" and once struck out twelve batters in a row, even kids older than himself. He could run and throw and field and was smart — baseball smart. And boy, could he hit. He led the camp in home runs, triples, doubles, everything. And then there was the story about the lake. Not even the grown-up counselors could hit a ball that far. But Johnson did — twice.

We believed every word Games said (why would he lie?), except the part about pitching like Bull. No one, I didn't care who he was, pitched that fast. Not John Johnson. Not anyone.

Games's story didn't surprise me. I could tell the minute I saw the new kid, even from the distance of my carport, that he was a ballplayer, probably a good one. His size was a giveaway. So were his strong-looking hands and arms. Games assured us of his coordination and eyesight. Then figure this: why would a kid who liked baseball, who was once a star player, give it up? Maybe he wasn't good anymore. Size, coordination, and eyesight weren't everything. You had to like to compete; you had to take the time to practice. A couple of kids I knew from school liked watching baseball but not playing. Maybe the new kid had become a watcher. Maybe.

Wart had an idea. "I bet his, er . . . religion d-doesn't allow it," he said.

"But he used to play," said AD, always a step ahead. "And what about his sister?"

"More'n likely it's got to do with his parents," I put in. "Bad grades and getting into trouble."

The others didn't say anything, but I knew what they were thinking. It was summertime. Bad grades could wait until the fall. As for trouble, the new kid, for all his size and mean-looking frown, didn't look the part.

Then what could it be? We needed a ballplayer bad, someone tough enough to combat Bull Reilly's blazing fast ball, to put him and his Hemlock Street pals in their place. We were a good team, better than good, but not quite good enough. At least not against the Poisons. The new kid was our answer — or was he? Maybe his sister, Olive, could tell us.

We practiced and played our home games on a field behind our houses. The field really wasn't a field at all, but two rows of backyards that bordered each other from adjacent streets. At the far end a highway ran due north, to the city; at the rear a clump of trees, the only ones in sight, cast a few yards of shadow and formed the backdrop for home plate. Gertie Gershwin's two-story drainpipe served as the left field foul pole, the whole of her house in fair territory; on the roof or over

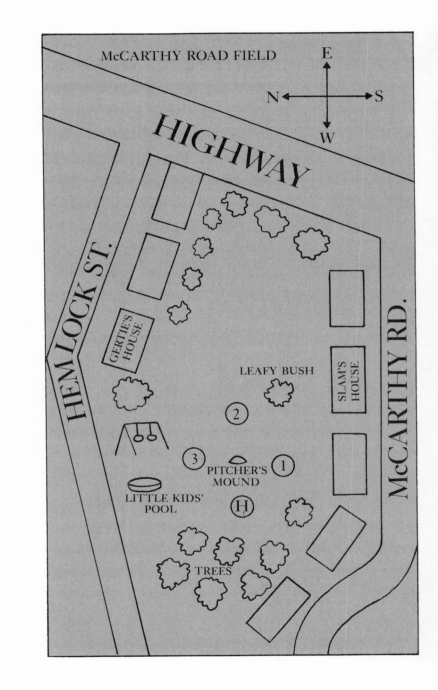

was a home run. A ball hit off the side of her house was akin, we imagined, to one hit off the Green Monster at Boston's Fenway Park.

Playing with a tennis ball instead of a hardball kept us from breaking too many windows. Center field, facing the highway, was open. Anybody playing the position had to be fast enough to cover a lot of ground. AD, our center fielder, could do that and more. He had a strong and accurate arm, and managed to pick up the flight of a batted ball despite being practically blind. Looking through his glasses was like swimming under-water with your eyes open.

To the right, Slam Sanders's house was a long poke. Only Slam himself, batting lefty, was able to reach it if he really got hold of one. The only obstacles on the field were a tall, leafy bush sprouting behind second, a few saplings too far away in left center to matter, and Gertie's backyard barbecue. In foul ground, behind third base, a family whose name I didn't know had put up a swing set next to an inflatable rubber swimming pool shaped like a turtle. Little kids were splashing in and out of it all day long.

Olive turned out to be a better player, far better, than any of us expected. (It seemed that being athletic ran in her family.) We tried her at second base, a vacant spot that Slam, our first baseman, had been trying to cover by shading over from his position. For somebody eleven years old, about to enter the sixth grade, a girl no less, she could field pretty well. Her style of fielding was to drop down on both knees and block the path of the bouncing ball with her skinny body, pick the ball up, then throw sidearm to first base. She glided rather than ran, with the grace of a long-legged deer.

Once I caught her doing a cartwheel when she should've been getting set in case the ball came her way. Instead the ball came my way and I missed it because I was watching her.

"Way to concentrate, Shooter!" Keyboard called in from left field.

My face turned red. The others laughed. Olive did another cartwheel.

When Games showed up to practice — surprise! — we broke into two groups and played a practice game, right field out of bounds. Olive had a little trouble fielding high pops (she ran in too far and they went over her head), but made up for it at bat, where she demonstrated the art of contact hitting, singles not home runs. She didn't strike out once, and even walked a few times, mostly because of the stooped-over way she batted, her head hanging out over the plate.

Afterward, we all went over to sit in the shade of the tree nearest home plate and wait for the ice cream truck, Mr. Jingles, to come down the street. All but Olive. As soon as the game ended she headed for her house. Maybe, being a newcomer, she was still a little embarrassed.

"Hey, Olive, wait a second!" I called out.

She stopped and turned around.

"Good playing today," I said. "Saturday's the game. Right here. Same time. Can you make it?"

She made a comical face like a bug-eyed fish, lips puckered, pink tongue darting in and out. In time I learned that this was the face she always made when she was thinking. Her baseball cap was tilted over her right ear. Her strawberry hair stuck out all over. Her T-shirt, with I GOTTA BE ME stenciled on the front, was soaking wet, her face dirty. She was as hot and sweaty as the rest of us.

"Yep," she finally said. "I think I can, unless —" She shifted her glove nervously from one hand to the other. "Unless . . . my mom and dad have something else for me to do."

"Try to make it," I said. "We need you out there. Ask your brother to come, too."

"I'll try," she said. "Me, that is, not my brother."

With that she turned a graceful cartwheel and was gone.

"Girls," Keyboard said, shaking his head.

"Yeah," said Wart. "Whadda we n-need her for?"

"Second base," I said.

"We got along without her up till now," Keyboard said.

"Yeah," I said. "Losing every game."

"Not every."

"Most."

"I don't know," said Keyboard. Still stretched out on the grass, along with Games and AD, he started to toss the tennis ball around. "Now, if it was her brother —"

"But it isn't," I said. "Not yet anyway."

"You got a plan?" Slam asked.

"I'm working on one. I'll let you know. Meanwhile, it's not as if we never had a girl play on the team before. Remember Betsy Whatshername?"

"She was older," Keyboard said.

"An' faster," said Games.

"Yeah," said Slam. "And boy, could she hit."

"She didn't wanna join our club, either," Keyboard said.

"Either will Olive."

"What makes you so sure?"

"She's younger," I said. "And . . . and there're other girls in the neighborhood. Just because she likes to play ball doesn't mean she wants to hang around a lot of guys. You saw. As soon as practice was over she split."

"Shy," said Keyboard. "See what happens when she's not."

"More'n likely," AD said, quiet all this time, "Shooter here will fall in love with The Cartwheel Queen and the two of them will live happily ever after."

4
The First
Game

As home team, we took the field in the top half of the first inning. Right away I could tell that Games, our pitcher, was set to have a good day. A lefty, he threw sharp breaking curves that popped in Wart's catcher's mitt, and a fast ball that looked good, too. Now if he could only last the whole game without tiring. Usually, around the seventh inning, we had to bring in Keyboard from left to relieve. Games would switch positions with him. We weren't nearly as good a team with Keyboard on the mound. Keyboard could throw fast enough; he just couldn't get the ball over the plate, ended up walking everybody, there'd be a key hit, and we'd lose. Also, Games out in left wasn't nearly as good a fielder as Keyboard. Come on, Games!

Slam, at first base, was tossing Olive and me some grounders, infield practice. Olive, who'd shown up without her brother, looked a little nervous, fielding the balls all right but throwing them back to Slam in the dirt. I bet she was surprised to see girls playing for the Poisons. I know I was, especially since I'd never seen either of them before — a chunky, older girl, with feet the size of footballs, and one a few years younger, who couldn't seem to stand still. I swear she had green hair. Not only that, but she was wearing a pair of sweat socks about ten sizes too large.

"Batter up!"

Charles J. Freedburg, shortstop, a kid I'd known since kindergarten, was first up for the Poisons. I moved a step or two toward third, Keyboard toward the left field drainpipe, er, foul pole. Freedburg was a strong pull hitter.

No matter. Games threw three quick curve balls right by him.

"You're out!" Wart hollered.

There was no argument; Freedburg had swung at and missed all three.

Playing sandlot, the catcher for each team (Wart for us, Tom Jefferson for them) had to double as umpire, calling balls and strikes behind the plate. All in all, it worked out okay. On any close play in the field we just argued, usually with the person who argued loudest winning. Even so, I can't remember a time when a game had been won or lost on account of an argument.

The Poisons had the older girl, Big Foot, batting second. She wore a baseball hat, too tight for her head, down over her eyes. She golfed Games's first pitch on a line to Slam at first. Two out. We threw the ball around the horn.

"Way to hum it, Games! Way to go!"

The third out was just as easy, a ground ball on one

hop back to the pitcher. Games fired it over to Slam and the Poisons' half of the inning was over.

"Way to go! Let's get 'em!"

Shooter Carroll, in person, was the Roaders' leadoff hitter. There were three broom-handle bats of different lengths to choose from (we always used broom handles when we played with a tennis ball), and while I picked one out I kept my eye on Bull. He was warming up with Jefferson, looking as huge, six feet tall at least, and ominous as ever. The day was hot, a scorcher, and already streams of sweat ran down the sides of his face and bare arms, arms about as muscular as my legs. His hair stuck out in dark wet curls beneath his hat. A morning's worth of dirt on his chin and neck made him look as if he needed a shave. He was thirteen years old, a year older than most of us, including me.

Without a doubt, Bull was the best pitcher any of us McCarthy Roaders had ever seen. He could throw the ball so hard that Jefferson had to use a special mitt with a sponge inside for extra protection. That is, when we were playing with a hardball. Tennis or hardball, the sharp breaking curve he threw, just for fun, started at your eyes and ended around your toenails. You were lucky if you fouled it off.

The pitcher's "mound," like the four bases, was just a patch of dirt, caused by the grass being constantly trampled. Strange as it might sound, none of the neighbors complained about their yards being torn up. The so-called field was so large that you hardly noticed the dirt spots anyway, which, except for third base, were way out in the middle. Once I'd heard my father say that the field was communal. That meant everybody used it. A lot of Edgewater Township (that's the name of our town), was communal, at least all the parks and playgrounds and town pool. Maybe that's why nobody put a fence around any of the backyards. AD knew another reason. "As renters," he had told me, "we're not allowed."

"Batter up!"

I stuck a new wad of bubble gum in my mouth, chomped down hard, and, taking a few practice swings with my broom-handle bat, stepped to the plate. To help anchor my back foot, I took a couple of seconds to dig a shallow hole with my rubber spikes the way I'd seen a lot of major leaguers do. I copied some of their other mannerisms, too. To loosen my back muscles, I held the bat at either end behind my neck and twisted around, left and right, straight up and bent over, like a gyroscope. I never played without a wad of gum in my mouth. Never. Chewing seemed to relax me and helped me to keep my mind on the game. When I was younger I pretended I was chewing tobacco and spit the juice all over everything, even my own spikes. All of us, as far as I knew, copied the styles of our favorite players. Not only that, but every time I ran onto the field I imagined playing before a big crowd at Comiskey Park. I bet the others did, too.

No matter how many times I faced Bull (six hits and one walk in more than forty at bats), I never got used to it. The huge muscle mountain — a mass of dirt and sweat — made me nervous, scowling fiercely at me from a pitcher's mound that suddenly seemed way too close. To make the game fairer, we should've made Bull pitch from out around second base, but you couldn't make Bull do anything. He did as he pleased. One thing I liked about him was that he never argued. He seemed to be above that. Oh, he'd scowl all right, swear under his breath, and I'd heard he once pounded a couple of kids who'd gotten in his way. But argue about baseball? Not since I'd known him. His teammates could argue; he'd pitch and hit. He hit the longest home run I'd ever seen on our field, clear over Gertie's roof, down her driveway, and into the street. It took us fielders about a half hour to find the ball underneath somebody's broken lawn chair, a block away, while Bull and the rest of the Poisons sat laughing at us in the cool shade of a tree.

"Strike one!"

The first pitch, a hard curve, faked me out completely. It started out at my head ("Duck!" my brain screamed), a spinning blur, then at the last second broke sharply over the plate, dead center. Sizzle-pop! Embarrassed, I picked myself up out of the dirt where I'd fallen.

"Knock him down again!" Jefferson bellowed. "He's nothin'!"

The rest of the Poisons picked up the chatter.

"Fire it in there, Bull! Fire it!"

He did. And — miraculously — THOWNK! I hit it, swinging late, on a line over Big Foot's head at first, toward the right field corner. I sped around the bases (if there was one thing I could do well it was run) and slid into third with a triple.

"Shoot-Shoot-Shoot-Shoot!" my teammates were

chanting. They gave me a raucous cheer, Keyboard the loudest. "WHOOP-DE!"

I tipped my hat in appreciation, spit some juice, and took a look at Bull, who seemed to be smiling. One measly hit wasn't going to wreck his confidence. He'd just play harder. I'd seen it happen before.

"Knock me in, AD!" I hollered.

AD was the perfect number two hitter. Choking up on the bat like myself, he almost always made contact. He could hit behind the runner, was a good bunter, and rarely struck out. He couldn't hit the ball as far as some of the others, but except for Slam and Keyboard, he was probably the best hitter on the Roaders. He swung at Bull's first pitch and lined one off the wall, beneath Gertie's kitchen window. BANG! I scored easily. AD had himself a clean double. We led, 1–0. Amazing!

Unfortunately, Keyboard, batting third, struck out. "Fungofandanglefat!" he screamed at himself, chucking his bat on the ground. Slam followed by hitting one weakly back to Bull whose wicked throw to first just about tore off Big Foot's glove. AD held second, where he watched Wart foul off a few before striking out on a ball pitched so hard it had a visible hop to it. No matter. We were ahead. And for a while that's how it stayed.

Olive led off our half of the sixth, with Games still pitching a shutout. She'd been up twice already, walking once on four balls at eye level (even Bull, who had great control, found it hard to pitch to her exaggerated crouch), and striking out looking. Even though she hadn't gotten a hit, she looked less awe-struck than I thought she would, tapping her bat on the plate, which was a square of wood, and staring with aplomb (one of AD's favorite words) at the pitcher. She had a funny way of wiggling her behind before she swung — I can't describe it — and I even saw her spitting once or twice in the dirt.

This time up at bat she barely had time to spit. On the first pitch she laid a perfect bunt single down the third base line. The Roaders, up on our feet, cheered her all the way to first. "Way to do it! Way to go!" Not that Olive was anywhere near finished, not at all. For on the very next pitch she stole second, beating Jefferson's throw by a long shot and shocking the heck out of the rest of us. When the dust had settled, Olive tipped her hat at us without looking.

Bull, meanwhile, bore down. He got me to ground out to second, Olive moving to third, where, after AD walked, she could score on a long fly ball, if only Keyboard could get hold of one. He couldn't. He swung and missed three times, dropped his bat disgustedly on the plate, and went over and sat by himself under a tree. He was too mad even to swear. It was Olive who brought him out of it.

In the blink of an eye, without warning and at full speed, she came hustling down the third base line, toward home. Bull saw her at the last moment, the same time Jefferson screamed for the ball. The pitcher fired it home, the runner, spewing up dirt and dust, slid head first. We held our breath, the catcher made a sweeping tag — too late. Safe! Olive had stolen home. The Roaders led by two. Make that four. A long home run by Slam onto the roof in right gave us a lead that seemed secure.

That's what we thought, anyway.

All this time Games was pitching his heart out, his best game ever. Inning after inning he'd kept the Poisons' big hitters off balance and off the bases. Big Foot had gotten a cheap single when AD misjudged her fly to center (I think the sun got in his eyes), and let it drop in front of him, and Freedburg had slammed one off the left field drainpipe for a double. But that was all, unless you counted the two errors Olive made on two pop flies, and two walks, both of them to Bull, who flied out his only other time up. Only six runners on base for the Poisons in six innings. Super!

The top of the seventh was a different story. Jefferson, up first, lined one off Games's shin for a single, which must've unnerved him because he walked the next two batters on eight pitches, a couple of them in the dirt. Like that — snap your fingers — bases were loaded with nobody out.

"Time!" I called out, trotting over to the mound from my position at shortstop. Slam and Wart, holding the catcher's mask in his hand, joined us.

"So, Games," I asked, "you losing it?"

He took his hat off and wiped his sweaty brow with his sleeve. His yellow cotton-candy hair shot out like a mess of uncoiled springs. He looked down at the ground — a bad sign — and shook his head. No.

"You sure?" I asked again. It was no time for fooling

around, not with the tying run at the plate. I didn't want
to bring in Keyboard to relieve, but I would if necessary.

"I'll be all right," he said in a whisper.

"Then settle down," Slam said. "A walk's a run."

"Sure," said Games, eyes on the ground.

Slam looked at me and shrugged.

"Let 'em hit it, Games," I said encouragingly. "We'll
do the rest." I gave him a pat on the butt and went back
to my position. One more batter, I said to myself. One
more chance and if he messes up, he's out.

But one more batter was one too many. Games's first
pitch to the Poisons' center fielder, a kid whose name
sounded like a dog's bark — Ruff — was hit on a line
onto the roof in left for a grand slam home run. An
inning later, facing Keyboard, Bull hit one over the
same roof. A small Roader rally fizzled out in the bottom
of the ninth, and that was that. Poisons 5, Roaders 4.
Our ninth loss in a row.

5
Yo-yos and
a Dead End

That Saturday afternoon, the same day we lost again to the Hemlock Street Poisons, a special event was to take place in the town shopping center, a place called The Plaza. The special event was a yo-yo contest, sponsored by The Wizard Yo-yo Company. Throughout the summer, every second or third Saturday, about fifty of us kids would congregate beneath the clock tower outside Sparkle's Candy Shack and practice yo-yoing while we waited for The Wizard to show up.

The Wizard was a wizened old guy, about a hundred years old, with a scrambled egg face — yellow and full of holes — and rotten teeth. No matter when you saw The Wizard, day or night, summer or winter, he was always wearing the same thing: a weather-beaten cowboy hat with the official Wizard "Big W" contest judge decal, and a matching denim jacket half-eaten by moths and covered with hairballs, lint, and splotches of bird doo, a jacket that was the envy of every kid who ever threw a yo-yo. Stuck to the outside of the jacket, too many to count, were the signs of The Wizard's accomplishments: decals representing all the yo-yo contests he'd won, from Mexico to Maine. The most, er, exciting one, a red square sewn over his heart, showed a photo of The Wizard when he was a little less bald, spinning two yo-yos at the same time, one in each hand, beneath a sign proclaiming him "County Fairgrounds Yo-yo King." He was flanked in the photo by a Jersey cow and a smiling girl with red lips, who looked all set to pop out of a string bikini. "Even the cow's got his eye on her," Keyboard remarked the first time he saw it.

All you had to do to enter the contest was own a Wizard yo-yo and show up at the right time, a half-hour or so before the Saturday movie matinee was to begin. The Wizard would limp up and down the long line of kids and watch each and every one of us do the pre-scribed tricks with our yo-yos. There were six tricks in all, going from easiest to hardest: Spinner, Walk the Dog, Rock the Cradle, Around the World, Donkey Ears, and Texas Star. If you missed even once — once — you were out. "Yo-yo, goodbye!" The Wizard would croak, like a dying bullfrog. See you later, and better luck next time. The three or four kids who managed to do all six tricks (never once me) went to the finals, which meant they got to appear on the movie theater stage, before about five hundred screaming kids, and do Loop-the-loop with their yo-yos until there was only one kid left, the winner.

The winner got to see the matinee for free. He got a "First Prize Wizard Yo-yo Contest" decal to sew on his jacket and a new Wizard yo-yo with an extra set of string. Best of all, he got his picture taken for the town newspaper alongside The Wizard, but — too bad! — not the cow and the bathing beauty. The kids who reached the finals but didn't win got second-place decals and a free seat at the movie.

My best effort so far, three summers' worth, had been to do five tricks in a row, the Texas Star keeping me from a place on the stage. "Five-trickers" were given runner-up decals, red cloth medallions in the shape of a yo-yo. I'd won three, but instead of getting my mom to sew them on my jacket I'd kept them in my bureau drawer. I'm not sure why.

That particular Saturday I happened to line up between my two friends, Games Murphy and Slam Sanders, two of the town's best yo-yoers. Both of them were frequent finalists, especially Slam. Ninety-degree weather didn't keep him from wearing his official Wizard Yo-yo Jacket, awarded him the summer before for beating the heck out of the rest of us, three contests in a row. Slam was a standout in other ways, too. He was, as you know, the McCarthy Roaders' first baseman and cleanup hitter. He was the tallest kid in the sixth grade, more than an inch taller than Keyboard, who I happen to know wears size large right down to his socks. Even with his friends, Slam was quiet, shy. It took him a couple of months after moving to the neighborhood before he'd answer anybody's questions with more than a single word or a grunt. "Yeah, mmm, nope." He was anything but lo . . . loquatious, unlike myself. One of the few black kids in town, he was liked by almost everyone who knew him, which says a lot. And, of course, he was a fierce competitor.

"Here comes The Wizard!"

I stopped practicing and so did everyone else as we got ready to show The Wizard that we'd mastered the first and easiest trick, Spinner. All it took was a simple flick of the wrist, just hard enough for the yo-yo to stop about an inch above the concrete and spin in place for the required five seconds before being jerked back up again. Easy. Or was it? Over my shoulder I could see The Wizard coming down the line, facing each contestant, now and then croaking out "Yo-yo, goodbye!" to the real beginners or to those who, for whatever reason, just messed up.

Suddenly my stomach felt like I'd swallowed a pizza, whole. I began to sweat like crazy. My fingers itched; my toes, inside my gym shoes, went numb. I guess you could say that, for me, competing in the yo-yo contest was in some ways worse than playing baseball against the Poisons and standing up at bat against Bull Reilly. No team would be behind me when my turn came, and I was none too confident. Come to think of it, there was something even worse than yo-yoing, which made me feel so bad I had to completely stop doing it. That was diving off the high board at the town pool, the Aquacenter. I was okay waiting my turn in line, but when I stepped out there all by myself, high above the blue-green water, and felt everyone's eyes on me, I choked. There's no other word for it. My lungs seemed to collapse like deflated balloons, so that I couldn't breathe; drops of sweat stung my eyes; my skin crawled with a million bugs. It was like being locked in a closet full of windows where everyone could see me but I couldn't see them, a terrible feeling when you happen to be about thirty feet in the air; everything, but especially the water, swirling about dizzyingly, while enough kids to fill a couple of buses keep yelling at you to do something, dive or jump, anything so they can get a turn. Funny, but I was a good diver, excellent, maybe, off the side of the pool, could even do flips and jackknives off the low board, but off the high board, forget it.

The last time I'd tried, last summer, turned out to be a disaster. Somehow I got out to the end of the board, but then I froze. My whole body came apart. The world spun around and around. And around. I shut my eyes, dropped to my knees and hung on for all I was worth. AD, next in line, and a couple of lifeguards had to rescue me, pry my hands loose and drag me back to the ladder, then help me down. It wasn't until my feet hit the pavement that I dared open my eyes. About a hundred kids were staring at me, laughing, as if I were some kind of looney.

"If I were you, kid," one of the lifeguards had said, "I'd stick to wading."

It was all so embarrassing. Never again, I'd promised myself. And for an entire year I'd kept my word.

The Wizard came limping down the line. For once, he'd taken off his official jacket. The day was too hot even for him, I guess. His bony arms, sticking out of an undershirt, were covered, from shoulder to wrist, with blue and red tattoos. There was a snake charmer blowing into a pipe before a coiled cobra, a wavy American flag, a skull and crossbones, and something that looked like a picture from Greek mythology. A Cyclops. A couple of greasy stains crept out from under The Wizard's pits. He was smiling his rotten-toothed smile. Games threw down his yo-yo, let it spin, and jerked it home. Now it was my turn.

Don't ask me what went wrong. Maybe it was the pack of cigarettes that popped out of The Wizard's undershirt pocket, startling me, just as I was about to throw. Or his weird underarm smell, like spoiled liverwurst. Or Games's sneezing (he had hayfever). Or my own horribleness. Whatever it was, I blew it. Down the yo-yo went and — Zip! — up it came again, without so much as a single spin.

"Yo-yo, goodbye!" the old bullfrog croaked. He gave me a look out of the corner of his eye, as if to say, "Another fool kid who probably can't even tie his shoes," and moved on to Slam, the kid yo-yo champion of all time — who also missed!

"Yo-yo, goodbye!"

"I don't believe it," Slam muttered to himself.

Games flashed us his wicked grin. "Gee, that's too bad," he said to the two of us, sarcastic as could be. I gave him a dirty look and went over to sit in the shade with Slam, where we could watch the rest of the contest. We weren't seated long.

It was in the middle of the very next trick, Walk the Dog, the one where you have to bounce your spinning yo-yo along the concrete before jerking it back up again, when something, somebody, on the far side of The Plaza caught my eye, a tall muscular kid with strawberry hair and a long stride. It was Olive's brother, John.

"Now where's he going in such a big hurry?" Slam wondered aloud. He'd seen the kid, too.

"Let's go and find out," I said, jumping up. "Maybe he'll even talk to us, answer a few questions."

"Doubt it. But it's worth a try."

We had to hustle to catch up. The kid cut across the park, past the movie theater entrance, and, almost running, beat a path along one of the crowded walkways, weaving in and out of all the shoppers, never once looking back, going toward one of the big department stores at the far end. Only he never got that far. All at once he took a sharp left through a door and into a building I'd never noticed before, a white brick building marked 33. That's all.

"Come on," I said to Slam. "We're gonna lose him."

Inside the door was a cool, dark hallway, with some stairs going up. We could hear the kid's footsteps on the stairs, moving slower now. No one else was around. I put a finger to my lips as a warning to Slam and up we went. The stairs creaked. Something scratched inside a wall. Ahead of us the kid's footsteps became faint. A door opened, then banged shut. Slam grabbed my arm and gave me a look as if to say, "Now what do we do?" I pointed up the stairs.

A narrow hallway with about a half-dozen doors on either side faced us at the top. The lights were out in all the doorways except two in the middle. Both doors were covered by sheets of frosty glass, so you couldn't get a look inside. On one of them, in black letters, was written ADAM ADAMS. Underneath, in smaller letters, was

PHILATELIST, whatever that meant. Inside, some people were moving about. You could see their shadows and hear faint voices behind the door. On the other door it said FRANCIS GEE, M.D., but except for the faint light the place seemed empty. There were no shadows, no voices. "Let's wait downstairs," Slam whispered.

I was all for turning the handles and opening the doors to look inside, especially that philyatelist, or whatever you call it, but, on second thought, Slam was right. Wherever the kid was, at the doctor or that other place, surprising him could end up embarrassing everybody. Besides, the kid'd know he'd been followed, probably get mad, and clam up even more. Then we'd never find out what was wrong, why he wouldn't play baseball. Downstairs, outside, we could pretend that we'd just bumped into him accidentally.

Slam and I hung around outside for as long as we could, maybe twenty minutes. A steady stream of people passed by on the walkway, adults, kids on bicycles, parents pushing baby carriages, old people, young, you name it, but not one of them entered the white building. No one came out either. In the distance we could hear the sounds of the yo-yo contest winding down — "Yo-yo, goodbye!" — and knew that if we waited any longer we'd miss the end, miss seeing if Games was one of the finalists, miss buying junk to eat in Sparkle's Candy Shack before the movie matinee started (this week's movie was *Frankenstein Meets the Killer Zombies*), maybe even miss the kids doing Loop-the-loop on stage, or, worse yet, miss the beginning of the movie. We just couldn't hang around any longer waiting for the kid to show. The mystery would have to stay unsolved.

"What's a philyatelist?" I asked Slam.

"You got me," was his answer.

6
A Pony League
Possibility

As it turned out, Slam and I did miss the rest of the yo-yo contest, at least the outdoor part. AD was waiting to tell us all about it outside Sparkle's, where we'd planned to meet.

"Where've you guys been?" he asked. "We're gonna be late."

"Tell you later," I said. "Who won? Is Games going on-stage?"

AD smiled broadly, pushed his glasses back on the bridge of his nose, above the Band-Aid, which looked like it was about to come unglued. He'd had the same Band-Aid on for days. "Sure is," he said. "Though he's not alone. There're two other hopefuls."

"Go get 'em, Games," said Slam.

"Oh, by the way," AD said, on our way into Sparkle's, "I couldn't find Wart. His parents' car was gone."

As for Keyboard, we all knew where he was, the same place he always was Saturday afternoon: at home practicing the piano. Once in a while, if we didn't have anything better to do, if there was no swimming or bowling or if the matinee got out early, we'd head on over to his house and stare at him through the living room window. Winter, summer, tornadoes, typhoons, the greatest day in the world — there he'd be, slobbering over the keys the way the rest of us slobbered over our dinners, his fingers and feet banging out a steady beat along with a metronome, one of those clickers that keeps time for music. Usually it was his mom or the same old witch piano teacher (we called her Squareyard) who'd be pressed up against him on the seat, coaxing him along. Outside, we'd make some small noises to distract him, get his attention, then make pignostril faces at the window until we'd get chased away.

Once I asked him why his parents made him play the piano.

"They don't," he answered. "I do it because I like to."

Wart, who was with me, and I looked at him in disbelief.

"Wouldn't you rather be playing ball?"

"Do fireflies pop when you squeeze 'em?"

"What?" said Wart, looking as puzzled as ever. "I d-don't get it."

Keyboard snorted. "I like to play ball — a lot," he explained. "Best of anything. But I like to play the piano, too, especially now I'm getting better."

"You sure could've fooled us," I told him. "About getting better."

The plastic bowling pin he was holding hit me square in the chest. The subject was closed.

Sparkle's Candy Shack, where we always went to load up on junk food before the movie, was small and spot-

lessly white, like a dentist's office, a single counter behind a long storefront window. Mr. Sparkle, the store
owner, was a bald guy with hair coming out of his ears,
muscular arms, and a friendly face. He came out of the
back when he heard the doorbell jingle.

"What'll it be today, boys?"

"It" was always a hard choice. The Sno-Kone machine in the corner, a giant silver box wet with condensa-
tion, looked inviting. For me, a Sno-Kone was a must on
a scorching hot day, but what else? I'd brought along
enough money to buy two or three things and still have
some left over for the movie. Games had slipped me
some money to buy stuff for him, too, in case he was a
finalist and had to head right for the stage when the
outdoor contest was over.

"Hubba Bubba," I said, coming to my senses. "Make
that two. Nerds. A cherry Sno-Kone, a pack of, er,
jawbreakers, three Milky Ways. No, wait. Snickers,
and . . . and one more thing." I snapped my fingers.
"An . . . an M&M's." The M&M's were for throwing
at the screen and at all the kids who'd be throwing
things at me.

While Mr. Sparkle was rounding up my order and
the orders of Slam and AD, the doorbell jingled and
some other kids wandered in, among them Tom Jefferson, the Poisons' catcher.

"Hey, pee-wee!" he shouted, the moment he saw me.
"Tough loss this A.M., huh?" He pushed his way through
the group of kids and came over to where I was standing.

"The name's Shooter," I said, as if he didn't know.

"Right," he said. "I forgot."

"Sure you did," Slam said.

Jefferson didn't pay him any attention.

"We'll get you next time," I said, sticking out my chest. His was a lot bigger.

"Right," said Jefferson. "Just like you did the last twenty times."

"Nine," I corrected him.

"Whatever you say," he said with a smirk.

He and his friends bought Sno-Kones and left.

"Excuse me," Mr. Sparkle said, handing me my bag of stuff. "I couldn't help overhearing. What did you lose this morning?"

I edged toward the door. So did Slam and AD. "A baseball game," I said, reluctant to talk about it.

"I didn't know Edgewater had summer leagues."

"It's only sandlot," I said. "Behind our houses."

"How often do you play?"

I shrugged and took a bite of my Sno-Kone. "Against the Poisons? Every Saturday morning, just about. All summer."

Mr. Sparkle looked impressed.

"Do you play Little League during the season?" he asked.

I nodded. The Sno-Kone had begun to drip over my hand, looking like a stream of blood, and I stopped to lick it.

"This was our last year," Slam said. "We're too old."

"So you'll play Pony League next year."

The three of us looked at one another.

"We could if we wanted to travel to Lorriesburg," said AD, speaking up for the first time. That was AD's way: size up the situation, make sure what you're going to say, then say it; it's like testing the water before you jump in. "Edgewater doesn't have a Pony League."

Mr. Sparkle's brow furrowed, as if what AD had said bothered him. He wiped a layer of sweat off the top of his bald head with a towel. The doorbell jingled and some kids started to come in but changed their minds and, laughing and calling each other names, went back out again.

"Why not play in Lorriesburg?" Mr. Sparkle asked.

"Who's going to take us there?" I said. "It's about ten miles away."

"And coach and manage?" said AD. "And be around for all the games and practices?"

I took a noisy slurp of my Sno-Kone, which was melting fast, even inside the air-conditioned candy store. Mr. Sparkle, using the same towel he'd used to polish his head, wiped off the counter.

"What about your dads?" he asked us.

"Shooter's dad works rotating shifts at the plant, or he'd probably do it," AD said, munching on a jaw-breaker. "Mine travels too much. Some fathers don't want to, mothers neither. A couple of us don't even have fathers, not around here. If we ended up having to forfeit a lot of games, it wouldn't be any fun."

Mr. Sparkle's brow furrowed again, like a plowed field, and his face screwed up in thought.

"If you had a Pony League in Edgewater, would that work?"

"We'd need someone to organize it," AD said, his mouth rolling along full speed now. "We'd need sponsors to buy the uniforms and equipment. Someone to keep the field in shape. Umpires. Probably more things than I can think of."

"I doubt that," Mr. Sparkle said with a smile. "How many teams do you suppose you'd have?"

The doorbell jingled and a woman carrying a baby in a backpack came in. "There're two junior high schools," I said. "Eight teams. Maybe ten if it was open to girls."

"Tell you what," said Mr. Sparkle, as he made himself a cherry Sno-Kone. "I'll look into the matter. Come back next Saturday and I'll tell you what I find out."

You bet we would. Pony League!

7
Dorp, Zombies, and Worse

Inside the movie theater it was noisy — kids were running up and down the aisles, scrambling for seats — and dark as a cave, with only the spotlights on the three yo-yo finalists brightening things up. The contest was already under way.

AD, Slam, and I, dropping a trail of candy as we went, found some seats up front, four of them. Above us, on the stage, Games and the other two kids were doing Loop-the-loops with their yo-yos, the last trick left to decide the winner. Loop-the-loop was simple. All you had to do was throw the yo-yo out in front of you underhanded, wait for the string to bring it back, then, without catching it, let it circle your hand and shoot out again, around and around. Games and Slam could do this trick about two hundred times without stopping. I'd seen them. Even I, no great yo-yoer, could manage fifty on a good day. On-stage, to win, you had to outlast the competition and be the last one "looping."

Games looked confident, the bright spotlights making his bush of yellow hair stand out like a bunch of furry wheat stalks. He was flicking his wrist expertly and had a good rhythm going. In and out his yo-yo zoomed, around and around in a circle. Next to him, a kid named Dorp was looking confident, too, although the baggy pants he was wearing, about ten sizes too large, resembled a couple of sleeping bags. He wasn't wearing a shirt and had a big roll of fat around his stomach. The other kid up there, whose name I didn't know, looked shaky. His arms seemed too long for his body and the loops he was making with the yo-yo kept getting slower and slower, until I was sure he was about to collapse, mess up, lose.

Instead it was Dorp who messed up.

His yo-yo must've hit his thumb on the inside curve. To compensate, he threw the yo-yo out hard, lost his balance, and, to the hoots and howls and screams of delight of hundreds of unruly kids, toppled over. He crashed all his weight into Games, whose yo-yo wound up on the floor of the stage, the string still attached to his finger.

Games, who had a firecracker temper, gave Dorp a scowl and a shove, hard enough to throw Dorp's weight the other way, on top of the kid with the long arms, the contest winner. Both kids went down in a heap, with Games jumping on top, trying to wind his yo-yo string around Dorp's nose. The Wizard, sweating so much he looked like he'd just stepped out of the shower, ran out from behind the stage and started dragging the kids apart.

Games was in a fury, angrier than he should've been. It was easy to tell. For one, he didn't want to let go of

Dorp's head, which he had in a headlock. Games wasn't grinning his stupid grin, a sure sign that something was wrong. And he was yelling out all sorts of things, swear words even worse than the ones Keyboard used. All of us had seen Games lose control like this before, at the — what's the expression? — drop of a hat, or in this case a yo-yo. "Games has a penchant for getting into trouble," my dad once told me, but he liked Games as did almost everyone who got to know him. Still, my dad warned me that when I was with Games I should be careful.

The problem was you never knew when Games was going to explode or, as Keyboard put it, "weird out." One second he'd be chatty and full of comedy, ready to do you the biggest favor in the world; the next calm and quiet, a good listener; the next crazy, out of orbit. He was moody and im . . . impulsive. That's the word. He never knew when to back off, stay put, cool it. "Think consequences," my dad was always saying. Games didn't. And he was always in the wrong place at the wrong time.

Trouble seemed to follow him around like a stray elephant, though the things he did that put him on the outs with his mother (his father lived in California) or the school principal or, sometimes, the police were more stupid than serious. Like the time he'd gotten a job delivering handouts for one of the local store owners. Instead of doing the job, he'd gotten bored and dumped what was left of the handouts down a sewer. Of course someone saw him do it. Or the time he got caught putting a litter of gray mice in the girls' bathroom at school, setting off firecrackers, chucking snowballs at cars, writing swear words in phosphorescent paint on the sidewalk in front of the police station, screaming in the library, running down the bowling lane after his ball (real lane, real ball) — the usual kid scrapes, only Games always got caught.

Games's mother's way of handling it was to load him up with work to do around the house. You name it, he did it, from vacuuming to babysitting for his little sisters, laundry to yard work. All the time he spent doing his chores, er, punishment, meant that he missed no end of fun: baseball practice, swimming at the Aquacenter, bicycle trips to the miniature golf course, as well as the hours spent down in my basement with the rest of the Basement Baseball Club. On Saturdays, game days, he must've done a whole lot of pleading to get his mother to give in. She couldn't keep him working all the time. Could she?

When The Wizard, with the help of the lady who ran the movie theater, broke up the fight — "Fight! Fight!" the audience was screaming — they quickly handed out the prizes (Games sailed his decal into the audience), took a picture of the long-armed kid with The Wizard, who looked ready to have a heart attack, and that was that. The lights on the stage went out and the movie began.

Our seats up front were perfect, including the extra one we'd saved for Games, except that he had trouble finding us in the darkened theater. We called out his name about twenty times, then practically had to tackle him as he came running up the aisle.

"Did you see that jerk Dorp?" he said disgustedly, scrambling into his seat. He was hot and out of breath.

"Shush!" I said. "Let's watch. I heard this movie is super."

That it was. Frankenstein, played by someone who had a face like a piece of raw hamburger meat and was as big as an NFL middle linebacker, was sleeping in a cemetery one moonlit night when the door to one of the marble tombs creaked open and out came a bunch of woodchuck-size rats and bats and insects, followed by about a dozen zombies, bug-eyed saucerheads. The zombies, already dead, were supposed to be indestructible. They stumbled around the cemetery for a while, arms out straight as sleepwalkers, until they came upon Frankenstein, scaring him right down to his size-twenty gym shoes. That's right, he was wearing gym shoes. The zombies, it was clear, wanted to eat Frankie for breakfast. He got away by climbing over the cemetery wall and flagging down a bus on the highway. A bus, in the middle of the night!

The best parts of the movie, other than that, were when the bus driver tried to make Frankie get off the bus because he didn't have any money; when the zombies were riding camels up and down a crowded street; when some friendly old ladies magically transformed themselves into witches, then plants, then back again to witches; and at the end of the movie, when all the zombies' heads fell off and Frankie and the witches sat around eating zombie stew.

Games didn't get to see the end. I guess losing the game and the yo-yo contest both in one day was too much for him. Whatever the reason, he acted awful, howling with laughter at the movie's scary parts, pretending to be scared at the funny ones. "Oh, no!" he'd scream. "Help, help!" Partway through the movie he accidentally-on-purpose dumped a box of popcorn on top of the girl's head in front of him, and got her own box of popcorn on top of him in return, followed by what was left of her jumbo-size Coke.

For that Games scared the heck out of her.

Here's what he did. He waited until there was a lull in the movie, a long silent part, when most of the kids in the audience were quiet, too, paying attention. I think it was the part where the witches were turning into man-eating plants. The gory special effects made it hard to take your eyes off the screen, which was why I didn't see Games get out of his seat and disappear in the darkness. When I noticed he was gone, it was too late. He'd already wound his way on his stomach across the pitch-black edge of the stage, ending up directly in front of the girl who, a few minutes before, had showered him with Coke and popcorn. There he lay, unseen, until exactly the right moment.

It came almost at once. The music got scary, the witch melted into a life-size plant, the hideous teeth of a zombie-monster filled the screen, the mouth slowly opened, and there was the start of an agonizing scream. Games, with his cotton candy hair, flashing grin, and screechy voice (making him a candidate for his own monster movie) suddenly jumped! "ARREEIIGGU-HLLAE!" he bellowed, arms and legs spread-eagled, as he landed an inch in front of the girl's face. I swear, she, her friends in the front row, and about forty other kids, including Slam, AD, and yours truly, practically died of fright right then and there. The girl who'd gotten the worst let out a bloodcurdler, loud enough to dent your eardrums, shot straight up out of her seat, and sped toward the exit for help, I guess.

She didn't have to go far. An usher, a bruisy looking guy about twenty, saw the whole thing. He and his flashlight were on Games in an instant. A second later, all by himself, he hauled Games away, kicking and shouting, up the aisle and out of sight. "Boo!" kids were yelling, but what could we do?

"Serves him right," Slam said. "What a maniac."

AD agreed, though by the look on his face in the dim light I could tell he was worried. I was too. What sort of mess had Games gotten himself into now?

"Be right back," I said, climbing over the others. But by the time I got to the lobby it was too late. Games was being led out the door toward a waiting police car.

When the movie ended, the three of us got on our bikes and headed for home. A familiar car sped past us, going in the opposite direction, barely stopping for the light at the Main Street intersection. The driver, Games's mother, didn't look happy.

"Pick-up time at the station house," said Slam. He was pedaling his undersized bike as fast as he could, trying to keep up with AD's and my three-speeders. "Games's in for it now."

"Afraid so," AD said. "Don't look for him to be out there on the mound next Saturday."

All I could do was shake my head. As if we didn't already have enough problems, what with Bull Reilly and the Poisons and the new kid who wouldn't play. Speaking of the new kid . . .

"Hey, AD," I said. "What's a phily-at-elist?"

"A what?"

"I think it's philyatelist."

"Philatelist," he said. "A stamp collector. Why?"

We were speeding along now, with Slam, pedaling hard, half a block behind. I told AD about following the new kid and where we'd ended up.

"Funny, but he doesn't look the stamp-collector type," I said.

"You mentioned two doors," said AD. "What was the other?"

"A doctor. Weird name. Something like M.D., Francis Gee."

AD slowed his bike down to let Slam catch up.

"He's a friend of my parents'," he said, giving me a hard look, as if he were about to reveal a dark secret. The wheels in his brain were spinning like mad. He shook his head knowingly.

"What?" I asked him, puzzled.

"Francis Gee, M.D.," he said, "is a shrink. A head doctor. A psychiatrist."

8
Playing to Lose

Wart was waiting for us down in my basement, eating a jumbo bag of potato chips, which he must have brought from home. He was hunched over a Monopoly board, rolling the dice, moving the markers around, handing out the cash and properties to the imaginary players, wheeling and dealing. Wart was famous for playing games by himself. Once he told me, in secret, that he found doing that more fun than watching TV or the VCR; he'd gotten in the habit when his family had lived way out in the middle of nowhere and there was no one else to play with, no brothers or sisters either. It seemed fine to me. I played Monopoly by myself, too, only I didn't tell anyone about it.

"Who's winning?" AD teased him, looking over the board. Wart, for all his huge bulk, was a grade behind the rest of us, Olive's age.

"I am," Wart said, without looking up.

We all laughed. It was hard not to.

"I guess it's kind of hard to lose when you're playing against yourself," I said.

He stuffed a handful of chips into his mouth. Mid-chew, he said, "I'm not . . . er . . . p-playing against myself. I'm this piece." He pointed to a silver thimble. "The other p-pieces are my op-opponents. See, it's his turn, hat's, to r-roll the dice. Now —"

The back door banged open, interrupting him, and Keyboard came down the stairs, wearing his bathing suit, his piano lesson over for another Saturday.

"Hey," he shouted, "what'd you say we —"

"Games's in jail," I told him.

He stopped in his tracks. A wet blob of chips popped out Wart's mouth and landed with a SLOP! on the Monopoly board.

"You're kidding," Keyboard said, when he'd re-covered.

He could see on our faces that we weren't.

"Fungofandanglefat!"

The three of us took turns telling Wart and Keyboard the whole story. When we'd finished, Keyboard asked, "Well, whadda we do now?"

"Lay low for a while," I suggested. "Give his mother a couple of days to calm down. We saw her on her way to the police station, probably to pick him up. When the time's right, one of us can go over to his house and see what's what. Until then we cool it."

It was agreed.

There was the rumble of thunder outside. The light coming in through the basement window had suddenly grown dimmer.

"Thinking of going swimming?" AD asked Keyboard, eyeing the bathing suit.

"I guess not. Maybe we can all go tomorrow."

"How about a game of Monopoly?" Wart suggested.

"Sure," I said. "But only if you get that disgusting blob of food off the board."

Like most games and sports (except baseball, which was fun enough on its own), we almost always played Monopoly for something — a root beer, a Sno-Kone, a pack of gum, a favor of some sort, losers buy winner. Today was different. Now that the excitement of the movie was over, it was hard not to think about that morning's loss, our ninth in a row to the Poisons, and our troubled team. The others must've had baseball on the brain, too. They were all quieter than usual, even Keyboard. It was Slam, good for an idea or two any day, who brought us out of it by suggesting that instead of the winner getting something, the loser of the game had to go over to the new kid's house to find out, once and for all, why he wouldn't play for us. "Get a straight answer out of him," were Slam's words.

AD shot me a look, no doubt thinking of the conversation we'd had just a few minutes before about the psychiatrist and all that. Still, I could tell that he thought Slam's idea was a good one. So did Wart and Keyboard. As for myself, I wasn't so sure. I wanted to find out about the new kid all right, probably more than the others; only what I'd learned earlier that afternoon made it clear to me that the whole thing had to be handled — what's the word? Diplomatically? Something like that. The new kid was as edgy as a base runner caught off the bag, and I didn't want to mess things up by being too nosy, too pushy. It was a situation that called for —

tact. That's what it's called. A tactful person knew when to go forward, when to back up. Knew enough to ask the right questions, without seeming too nosy, someone who didn't step on anybody's toes. Someone easy to trust. Wart, Slam, Keyboard, even AD, good friends all, for one reason or another, weren't right for the job. Only one of us was — me. Now all I had to do was go against my natural instincts and play the Monopoly game to lose.

"Your turn," Wart said, handing me the dice.

"Who won the yo-yo contest?" Keyboard asked.

"Some sucker," said Slam. "Games was second."

"What about you?" Keyboard said. He eyed Slam's official yo-yo jacket, with all the fancy decals he'd won.

"Never mind."

I rolled the dice and took my turn. The others did the same.

"Why get so dis-disgruntled over a yo-yo contest?" AD said out loud, to no one in particular. AD wasn't the least bit interested in yo-yoing.

Slam and Wart gave him a look.

"Or chess," Keyboard said.

"There's a difference," said AD, collecting his two hundred dollars for passing "GO." "It has to do with — maturity." Behind his glasses, his dark eyes lit up like two hot charcoals. He liked poking fun at the rest of us.

"And coordination," Slam said.

"And . . . spirit," said Wart.

"Spirit?" AD thought about this for a moment as players' markers hopped around the board. "You could be right," he said.

Listening to the others, I thought so, too. Only I'd have added confidence. Slam and Games felt confident yo-yoing, AD playing chess or fiddling with his computer, anything where he could use his brain. Maturity? Now that I thought about it, I could see AD's point, also. I guess I was feeling a little too old to be playing with yo-yos, while some old fart with sweaty pits, tattoos, and a cowboy hat croaked, "Yo-yo, goodbye!" and other nonsense right in my face. Maybe that's why I kept my decals hidden in my bureau.

The game heated up. Monopoly dice and markers moved around the board, money changed hands, properties were bought and sold. There were, as usual, a few arguments ("You don't collect two hundred dollars when you go directly to jail." "You owe me rent." "Move nine, not ten."); a few acts of trickery by the designated banker, AD; a few shady deals among the participants ("I'll sell you this, if you sell me that"). We chased my little brothers back upstairs when they tried to join us, then conned them into bringing us a big pitcher of ice water and some glasses. Every now and then I could hear my mother and her friends playing bridge or mahjong in the room above us. The basement was cool and comfortable. Outside there was a clap of thunder.

"My offer from the other day still stands," said AD. "A pack of gum if you can name five former players, major leaguers, with animal nicknames."

"Do birds c-count?" Wart asked, taking his turn.

"I guess so," AD said.

"Er . . . Mark 'The Bird' Fidrych," Wart guessed.

"That's one," AD said.

Wart moved his marker around the board. "Anything else to eat?" he asked. We'd finished off his potato chips.

"Check with my mother," I told him.

"Tater Scott," said Keyboard, who'd been thinking hard.

"That's a vegetable," AD said, deadpan, not looking up from the board. "Whose turn?"

The rest of us let out a laugh, even Keyboard. Suddenly I got a brainstorm. "Ducky Medfield," I said.

"That's Med*wick*," said AD, smirking. "Though it's easy to see how your mind works. Duck, field. Very associative."

I wasn't amused, but the others were. "WHOOP-DE!" Keyboard hollered. Wart got up to go upstairs.

"Your turn," AD said to me. "And by the look of things, you're just about out of money and properties. You're on the verge of going down the tubes in defeat." His eyes sparkled. He knew what I was up to, playing to lose. I knew he knew it, and he knew I knew he knew it. AD was always one — or several — steps ahead of me. He also knew I was probably the best person to learn the truth about the new kid. If he had to, he'd have rigged the game so that I'd lose, no matter what. Don't ask me how. He'd have done it. As it turned out it wasn't necessary. Keyboard, Slam, and Wart — all three of them had played their hearts out, not wanting the scary task of confronting a kid who looked strong enough to rip their arms off.

"Wasn't there a 'Rabbit'?" Slam asked, getting back to nicknames.

"Right!" said Keyboard. "I think it was Rabbit Maranville, something like that."

AD gave the two of them a look of mock disgust. "I see I'll have to make the questions harder," he said. "Name two more."

Wart returned from upstairs with two handfuls of saltines. A short time later, when we couldn't guess (remember Catfish Hunter, Moose Skowron, and . . . Bulldog Bouton?), AD told us to keep thinking about animal nicknames. He told us that there were thirty or forty to choose from. In the end, I lost the Monopoly game by a wide margin.

"When will you talk to Johnson?" Keyboard wanted to know.

"I wanna watch the Sox game on TV tonight," I told him. "So before then. After dinner."

"Let me know what happens," he said.

"Me too," said Wart.

"Me too," said Slam.

"Good luck," said AD.

Gee, thanks.

9
Chocolate Pudding and the News

The new kid's mother opened the porch door when I rang the bell. She was tall, giraffe-like, with a white face full of freckles and a mound of dark red hair piled on her head that looked ready to topple off at any moment. The hair, that is, not the head. There was no guess about who her kids took after.

"You must be Shooter," she said.

"Wh ——— !" I was so surprised I practically fell down. She noticed.

"Olive's told us about you," she explained. "I'll go get her."

"N-no," I stammered. "John. I'm here to see John."

"He's out with his father," she said, pushing open the screen door. "But Olive's home. Olive! Shooter's here!" Under her breath, she said, "She'll be so glad to see you."

Oh!

Olive came bounding down the stairs, pushed past her mother and out onto the porch. "Hi," she said, a squeak. "Come to talk strategy?"

" 'Strategy'?"

"For next Saturday's game. There is one, isn't there?"

"There's a game, all right," I said. "Same time, different field. Over on Hemlock Street."

"I can't wait."

"Listen, Olive —" I began, but she cut me off.

"I've been thinking," she said.

"Thinking? Of what?"

"Wanna sit down?"

"Er . . . no," I said, sidling backward. "Tell me what you were thinking."

She looked at me with her vanilla cupcake face. At night her nose and hair didn't look as red. She had a long scratch and puffy bruise on her chin, probably from sliding into home headfirst that morning. The memory of it made me smile. I took a deep breath and hitched up my pants.

"We might change the line-up," Olive said tentatively, "Of course, that'd be up to you — and the others."

"Change the line-up? How?"

"You've got whatshisname, Keyboard, batting third. I think that's wrong."

"Wrong? He's our best hitter," I said.

She stared at the floor, at her feet. She was barefoot.

"I don't think so," she said. "Not against Bull Reilly."

I was about to argue when the screen door swung open and Olive's mother came out with a couple of dishes of chocolate pudding with whipped cream on top.

"You two sit down and have some of this," she said. "John'll be home soon."

What else could I do? There were a couple of wicker

chairs in the corner, across from a porch swing. I sat in a chair and dug in. The pudding was soft and chocolatey, smooth, warm, delicious.

"And another thing," said Olive, in between bites, "we could —"

All at once it hit me. Olive was such a good talker, maybe . . .

"What's wrong with your brother?" I asked her.

She kept on popping the spoon in her mouth and didn't say anything. I counted to about twenty before I said again, "What's wrong with John? Why won't he play ball?"

"I can't tell you," she said, staring down at her feet. I noticed that her big-toenails were painted light pink.

"Why not?"

"Just can't. It's a secret . . . sort of."

"Games's right. He's a good player, isn't he?"

"He's the best!" she blurted out. She tried to look my way, but looked out at the darkened street instead. A car went by. I could hear Keyboard yelling way down at the end of the block.

"Come on, Olive, you can trust me. Ask anyone."

"You'll tell the others."

"Not if you don't want me to."

"So you say."

All at once, like a kernel of popcorn, she was up and gone, taking the two empty pudding dishes into the house. I waited for what seemed a long time, but probably no more than five minutes, not knowing if she was coming back out or not. Every so often a car, headlights on, would go by on the street. If I listened hard I could hear a group of younger kids, my brothers among them, playing flashlight tag. "Missed me! Missed me!" The Sox game would be starting soon. In anticipation, I stuck a wad of gum in my mouth. "One more minute," I said to myself, "then I'm leav ——"

The screen door banged open and out came Olive, holding something in her hand. A slip of paper.

"Promise not to tell?" she said. "My brother'd kill me."

"Promise."

She almost threw the piece of paper at me. It was a newspaper clipping. There was just enough light on the porch for me to read it. Here's what it said.

Boy Hurt in Game

Quincy, N.Y. — Benny Patch, 12, of Rice Road was injured during a Little League baseball game Saturday when he was struck in the head by a pitched ball. He was taken to St. Vincent's Hospital where he is listed in critical condition.

I looked at Olive and shrugged. None of it made sense to me.

"My brother John was the pitcher," she explained.

"So?" I still didn't get it. Olive didn't say anything, and then it dawned on me.

"You mean . . . he hit this kid, Benny Patch, in the head. And they had to take him to the hospital. And now your brother won't play baseball anymore. Because he's ——"

"Scared," said Olive.

"I see," I said slowly, only I didn't. Not yet.

Olive stared at me, kind of nervous, hopping from one foot to the other. I got the feeling she wasn't clear about all this either.

"What happened to Benny?" I asked her. "Did he die? When was this, anyway? Why wasn't he wearing a batting helmet?"

"It was last year. He was wearing a helmet, but the ball hit below it, near his ear. No, he didn't die. But he had to get a metal plate put in his head. And he can't play baseball anymore. Not ever. He was in the hospital a long time."

"And you brother's scared that'll happen to him?"

Olive's eyes bugged out, her lips puckered like a fish, and she stuck out her tongue. She put her hands on her hips. For a second I thought she was going to yell at me.

"You're not too smart, are you?" she said. "John's not scared of getting hurt. Look how big he is. He's scared of hurting someone else. Some other kid. He was the fastest pitcher for his age anyone ever saw. My dad even says so."

"A year ago?" I said, still perplexed. "And your brother's never pitched, never played baseball since?"

"That's right," came a deep voice from behind the screen door. It was John.

10
Two Strikes and You're Out

The screen door swung open. If anything, the new kid seemed even more imposing than before, tall and square, his yardstick shoulders taking up most of the doorway, though I'd found out from Olive that he was only a year older than I was, about to start the eighth grade. His face had a mean-looking frown; his eyebrows twitched.

He came over to where the newspaper clipping had fluttered to the floor in between Olive and me, picked it up without looking at it, and shoved it inside his back pocket. I braced myself for the worst.

"Why'd you have to go and tell him, Olive?" the kid said, his voice a whole lot calmer than I expected. He looked more sad than angry.

"There's nothing to be scared of," I blurted out, before I could catch myself.

The kid looked down at me. "A lot you know," he said.

"It could've happened to anyone," I said cautiously.

"But it happened to me. And Benny, the kid I hit."

"It'd probably never happen again."

"I can't take that chance."

Suddenly it dawned on me.

"You couldn't hurt anyone playing in our game," I said. "Not even pitching."

Olive's face brightened up. She'd gotten it, too.

"That's right," she squeaked. Her voice sounded like a skinny balloon that'd let all its air out in a rush.

"Why is that?" John asked. I could tell he didn't believe us.

"Because," Olive and I said at the same time, "we play with a tennis ball!"

The kid shoved his hands inside his pockets and stared at us. He smiled warily, his eyeballs shifting nervously. His face was as wet as a steam bath.

"You . . . you can . . . hurt people in other ways, too," he stammered. "Not just beaning them."

I didn't understand what he was saying.

"You mean hurt their feelings?"

"Hurt them — physically," he answered. "Putting somebody's eye out with a baseball hat. Running into them on the base paths. Spiking them."

"Accidents happen," I said.

"The trick is to avoid them — the situations."

"I'd never give up baseball," I said, the truth.

The kid started to say something else, but stopped himself. Olive just stood there, shifting her weight from one bare foot to the other.

"Come watch us play," I suggested. "Watch Olive. You were right. She is good." Olive blushed, her strawberry nose ripening. "You could even umpire. Anything."

The kid didn't say another word, but I thought his head moved back and forth a fraction of an inch — no. "Why —"

But it was no use. A second later he was back inside the house, the screen door slamming behind him. Strike one! I said so long to Olive, who gave a little shrug (what more could we say?) and ran off to watch the Sox game.

The week to come was pretty slow. I was anxious to practice, as were the rest of the Basement Baseball Club, but it rained almost every day, and when it wasn't raining the field was too wet to play on. As it turned out, we spent most of the week in my basement, competing against each other in just about every game we knew. We held tournaments, awarding points for coming in first and second. At week's end, whoever had the most points would win first prize, a jumbo bag of miniature Milky Ways, which the rest of us would chip in to buy. Second prize was a pack of sugar-covered doughnuts. Whoever did the worst and came in last place had to do a chore for every other contestant (my main chore around the house was mowing the lawn), the booby prize. More like a punishment if you ask me. At any rate, I'm sure you'll agree, no one wanted to lose.

Monday, the first of three straight rainy days, we held a marathon dice-baseball tournament, a game we'd made up ourselves, using rolls of the dice to determine outs, hits, runs, and errors, inning by inning. It was one of the club's favorite games and, because it was based entirely on luck, hotly contested. Tuesday morning we bowled, using the plastic pins and ball set-up in my basement — a good game, except that we got too rowdy, especially Keyboard, who let loose a couple of "Zapashucamarmalades!" every time he messed up. My mom made us calm down to Monopoly, Parcheesi, and round-robin chess, which AD won easily. It was either calm down or, in my mom's words, "vacate the premises."

The next day, my mother's day off from work, she treated us all to a couple of rounds at the Edgewater Township Bowling Lanes, mostly, I guess, to get us out of the house.

Before heading off to the bowling lanes with the rest of the guys, AD and I paid Games a visit. More than three days had gone by since his trouble with the law, high time to find out what was what. Had he spent a night in jail? Was he barred from yo-yo contests, from ever again stepping foot inside the movie theater, from horsing around with his friends? Most important, could he pitch in Saturday's game? None of us had seen him since he'd been hauled away inside the police car, not even outside his house, doing yard work, as usual, for his mother. I'd called him on the phone a couple of times, but his mother wouldn't let me talk to him. Was she still mad at him?

She was, and then some!

"No, Shooter," she told us at the back door. "He's busy working, and you and AD can't come in." She sounded tired.

"We just want to talk to him a second, Mrs. Murphy," I said, as reasonably as I could. "About Saturday's game."

"Paul won't be playing." Mrs. Murphy always called Games by his real name.

"Not playing? But he's got to, Mrs. Murphy. He's —"
I got flustered and forgot what I was going to say. Part
of the problem was that Games's mother had stepped out
on the back steps. To use Keyboard's words, she was
"scintinabulous, about as foxy as they come." For a while
I wasn't exactly sure what he meant, though, of course,
I'd never told him that. Lately the message was coming
across loud and clear. She was like something out of a
movie magazine, frizzy blond hair and a lot of lipstick
and tan like you wouldn't believe. Big muscles, too,
probably from all that jogging she did and the races she
ran in. She was the only person — the only lady — I
knew who was a match for the bathing beauty on the
yo-yo Wizard's jacket decal.

"He's our only pitcher, Mrs. Murphy," AD put in,
when I couldn't find the words. "And the game's a big
one. Real big."

"They're all big ones, AD," said Mrs. Murphy, with a
lipstick smile. "I'm sorry, but you'll just have to do without Paul. He's grounded."

"For how long?"

"Until he proves to me that he can be trusted. A long
while."

"But —"

"Sorry. No phone calls either."

Strike two.

After bowling, the rain having let up for an hour or
so, we all played flies up in the street, watching out for
cars and delivery trucks, bicycles and baby carriages,
keeping track of how many catches everybody made to
decide a winner. Then, in the last stages of the tourna-

ment, we settled on dart-throwing indoors, which I won, and a bicycle race outdoors, which Keyboard won to finish first overall, the proud owner of a jumbo bag of miniature Milky Ways, enough to last him — or anyone — a couple of weeks. Slam finished second, AD and I third and fourth, out of the prize money. Wart came in last, mostly because one of his darts ended up stuck to the basement ceiling and because, on the far turn of the bicycle race, he'd run into some garbage cans, scattering moldy food and junk all over the street.

For the booby prize, Wart's list of chores included mowing my front lawn, washing Keyboard's family's car, pulling all the weeds in the Sanderses' garden, and helping AD's father make bread (he was happy and so was Wart who, as you know, ate like a rhinoceros). He also had his own chores to do, which made him miss practice on Friday, but that didn't matter. What with one thing and another — dentist appointments, piano lessons, jobs, trips to the city with parents — the Basement Baseball Club was scattered all over. It turned out AD and I were the only ones around.

"So," AD said to me, "is the new kid going to play or isn't he?"

"Like I told you all before, how should I know?"

We were out at the field, playing catch with a hard ball, the soft throws landing in our gloves with gentle whaps. Nearby, in back of my house, my little brothers were digging in their sandbox with a couple of the neighbors' kids, squeaking away, throwing shovelfuls of sand over their heads, like they were shooting it out of a toy cannon.

"Still not going to tell your best friend?" AD called out.

"I told you. It's a secret. I promised. And don't let on about the psy — chiatrist, okay?"

AD snorted, the bandage on his nose flapping in the breeze.

Not telling the others about the news clipping had been a hard promise to keep. I got pestered to no end, especially when I didn't know whether the new kid had changed his mind or not about playing. "He's got a good reason not to," was all I said. And, "Anything's possible."

Sure, anything, like a snowman Santa Claus landing a reindeer-powered UFO on my roof.

Whap! Whap! Whap! Whap!

The ball AD and I were throwing sailed back and forth.

"Olive wants to change the line-up," I called out.

"Figures," he said. "A girl. One game and she takes over."

"It's not like that —" I started to say, but he fired the ball over my head and I had to run to get it.

11
Game Two, Part One

The place where we played baseball behind Hemlock Street was anything but a baseball field. Oh, there was an infield, all right, just like we had on McCarthy Road, dirt bases, home plate, a spot for a pitcher's mound; same dimensions, too. The problems were the "tot-yard," the nearby highway, the steeplechase outfield, and a few other things you had to worry about.

All the way around, the outfield was small, with buildings on every side, kind of like Boston's Fenway Park with three Green (in this case red-brick) Monsters. As on our street, the buildings were two stories tall, except that by being so close to home plate they made hitting a home run even harder. You'd think that the smaller field would make for more home runs, but in order to hit one out on Hemlock Street you had to "sky" the ball, uppercut it, so it would clear the wall. My teachers in school would call that a . . . paradox. What always happened was that long pop-ups on our field were home runs on Hemlock's, line drive rockets were singles, the tennis ball richocheting off one of the brick walls or windows and bouncing back to the infield. The bigger guys, like Keyboard and Slam on our team, didn't like the Poisons' field at all. They were robbed of too many good hits. As for me, who had a natural uppercut and not as much power, I liked it fine, the short fences, that is.

What I didn't like nobody liked: the obstacles. Ten yards behind second base the grass ended where a narrow road allowed cars in and out of a small parking lot stuck in the middle of right field. There wasn't much traffic — just enough to delay the game four or five times an hour — but the traffic wasn't the problem. The curbs on either side of the road were. So far I'd tripped over them only about a hundred times, chasing after a fly ball or a pop-up, practically killing myself on the concrete. Down the line in left was the tot-yard, a roomy playground for the little kids in the neighborhood, surrounded by a chest-high wooden fence. Anything hit inside the tot-yard was an automatic ground rule double.

Another problem, since the field faced the backs of the buildings, was that just about everything people owned and were used to keeping outdoors was in play: barbecues, outboard motors, plastic wading pools, a badminton set, garbage cans, winter sleds, clothes lines, lawn chairs, even an upright piano. ("You can play ball and practice your scales at the same time," AD told Keyboard.) The trick for the outfielders was to dodge the mess. Ever try catching a fly ball while leaping over a flaming barbecue and about a dozen scorched hamburgers? Probably not.

Last but not least was the highway, a short distance — too short — behind the catcher, who had to make

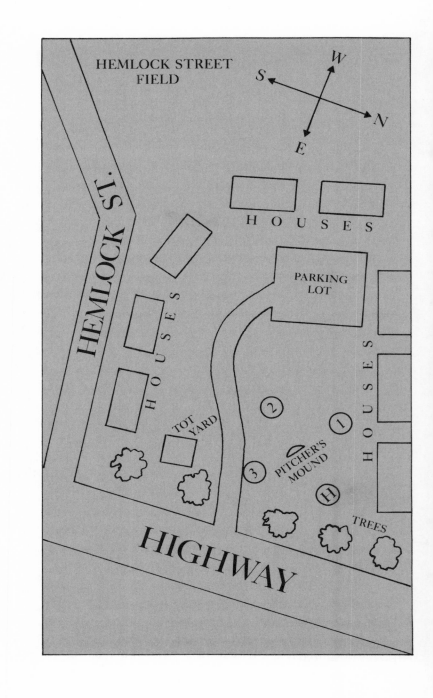

doubly sure to hang onto the ball. If the pitch got by you and rolled onto the highway, anybody on base was sure to score. Worse yet, the tennis ball could easily get squashed. We always brought along two or three extra balls just in case.

The Poisons took the field in the top of the first inning. Strange, but I knew the day was going to be something special the moment I woke up that morning and saw the hot summer sun (not rain!), baseball weather, coming in through my bedroom window. I was right. Bull Reilly was missing. "He's at the dentist — emergency," Jefferson grumbled when asked. He added, "We don't need him. We'll whip you anyway."

Just about everybody on our team, including AD, was disappointed. We'd never beaten the Poisons with Bull playing, and now we'd have to wait even longer to get the chance. "It'll be a hollow victory," I heard AD mutter to nodding heads. I sort of felt that way, but not completely. Bull or no Bull, most of all I wanted to win.

Showing my best stuff, I hit the first pitch thrown by Mickey Mudd, the Hemlock's regular right fielder, now pitcher, off the chimney in left field for a home run. McCarthy Road, 1–0! But that wasn't all, not by a long shot.

Before our half of the first inning was over we led, 5–0. Right from the start Mudd was wild. My home run must've bothered him because he walked AD and Keyboard (I hadn't changed the line-up) on eight pitches before Slam, batting left-handed, smashed one on a line off somebody's back porch railing in dead center for a triple. The kid whose name was Ruff robbed our next

batter, Keyboard's younger brother, Ping, who was filling in for Games, of an extra base hit by diving into some
pachysandra to come up with the ball. Slam tagged up
anyway and scored. Wart got hit with a pitch on the rear
end ("That's using your brain!" Keyboard chortled).
Olive struck out, over-swinging at a pitch that bounced
in front of the plate. Up for the second time, I hit what
should've been the third out on a hop back to Mudd, but
in his hurry to make the play, he fired the ball ten feet
over Big Foot's head, and I made it to second, Wart to
third, still with two outs. AD followed by laying down a
perfect bunt for a run-scoring single, and it was 5–0. As
it turned out, Ruff had to make another nice catch against
the center field wall to take away a sure hit, this time by
Keyboard, to end the inning.

Our turn to take the field.

Freedburg, as usual, led off for the Poisons, and before
his turn at bat was over I knew we were in for a long
day, a real dog fight. Like Mudd, Keyboard, our starting
pitcher, was wild, walking Freedburg on four pitches.
This was nothing new for Keyboard, who threw hard,
but was as wild as a wasp in a spider's web. Without
Games, Keyboard was our only hope.

Ruff followed Freedburg at bat. Keyboard walked
him, too. "Way to pitch, ace! Try your other arm! Try
underhand!" The Poisons were giving it to him. The
loudest mouth was Tom Jefferson. He really had it in for
us, worse than any of his teammates. Razzing, trying to
psyche the other team out, name-calling — it was all part
of the game. We McCarthy Roaders did it to them, so

why shouldn't they do it to us? They should, except that Jefferson went bananas, whistling and screaming when we were on the field, insulting us at bat ("No batter, no batter, chump, chump!"). He was even worse when Bull wasn't around, and I'm not sure why. In a way he seemed nervous, biting his fingernails down to the knuckles, never sitting still. Maybe he was angry about something. Maybe I was. After all, he did call me "pee-wee," didn't he? The name made me squirm.

Fights were another thing. Slam and Keyboard, at one time or another, had mixed it up with Jefferson, Keyboard more than a few times, at school even. I'm not exactly what you'd call impartial, but I thought that Jefferson had started more than his share. Even today . . . well, you be the judge.

It all started Jefferson's first time at bat. Freedburg was on second, Ruff on first (remember the walks?), with one out. Jefferson stepped to the plate. "Strike the loser out!" I hollered at Keyboard from my position at short. My teammates picked up the chatter, like they were supposed to do to give the pitcher some encouragement. "Make him hit it! Way to fire! No batter!"

Jefferson worked the count to 2–2. He was a pretty tall kid, square as a concrete block and muscular, with a big rear end like Wart. He didn't run very fast, but was tough behind the plate, hard to knock over. I know because I'd tried and failed a lot of times.

On Keyboard's next pitch, Jefferson hit a looping fly ball over first, toward the parking lot. AD, who had to cover both center and right, had a long run, picked the ball up on the bounce, and fired it in to me, where I was covering second. Jefferson, rounding first, came lumbering toward the bag, like a steam engine going up hill. AD's throw was a little up the line, into the runner. The ball and Jefferson arrived at the same time. We crashed, hard — UNGURFF! — Jefferson trying to slide under me and knock me off my feet, which he did, and the ball from my glove. I swallowed my gum, but hung on, landing on top of him, my elbows banging his face.

"You're out!" I screamed at him, leaping to my feet.

"The hell I am!" he hollered back. "You never tagged me, pee-wee!"

"The hell I didn't! And don't call me pee-wee, bacon-butt!"

He hit me before I could hit him, or try to. We wrestled each other to the ground, kicking and scratching in the dirt. His knee banged my rib cage, his head my chin. I shut my eyes and wailed away with both hands, my right one hitting something hard — his forehead — my fingers, hand, arm going instantly numb. We rolled over a couple of more times and then someone yanked me off. Keyboard, I think.

"Come on, let's play ball!"

"Break it up! It's only the first inning!"

AD had a big smile on his face. A couple of the Poisons were holding onto Jefferson, who was rubbing his forehead.

"Call it a draw," Slam said.

A few of the others laughed. I didn't see what was so funny.

"You're out, bacon-butt," I said, giving him my best stare.

"You never tagged me," he said, staring right back. "Chicken pee-wee!"

"Who's a chicken?"

"You are."

"Name your time and place," I said, feeling my knees go slightly weak. My voice had become a croak. So had Jefferson's a little bit.

"Right after the game," he said. "No wait. Got me a better idea." He stopped rubbing his forehead and his face took on a lopsided smile, almost a sneer. "Next time you're at the Aquacenter, meet me at the high board. We'll see who's a chicken or not." He laughed out loud.

Somehow he'd found out about my problem. Maybe he'd been at the pool the day the lifeguards had to rescue me from the end of the diving board.

"You're on," I said, as cool as I could be, though I was anything but. The thought of the high board sent a pricker-bush feeling up and down my back.

He snickered. "And I'm still safe."

"He's right, Shooter," Slam said, when I started to protest.

"No two ways about it," Keyboard agreed. "And while you were fighting two runs scored. But that's okay. I'd pay to see you fight anytime."

"Gee, thanks," I said.

"Great job," said AD.

I went over to my position at shortstop. Across the diamond Olive winked at me. She was smiling, too. I gave her the same scowly look I had given Jefferson to make her stop. She stuck out her tongue, then turned a cartwheel, right there, midway between first and second, as Keyboard was about to deliver the next pitch. A cartwheel, graceful as could be.

12
A Sudden
End

The game picked up exactly where it left off, Roaders leading, 5–2, Jefferson on second with nobody out. On the first pitch Jefferson stole third because no one, meaning me, was covering. We only had seven players, which meant that AD had to shade toward right in the outfield, while I shaded toward third in the infield. It was a lot of territory for both of us to cover. I was used to it, but Olive's cartwheel and my hurt hand, which was starting to swell up, had made me lose my concentration. So had thinking about going off the high board at the Aquacenter.

"Wake up out there!" Wart called out.

I did, or tried to.

Big Foot, the Poisons' first baseman, used a tiny bat for someone so big, holding it upright behind her ear and whipping it around like a golf club at the low pitches, missing the high ones by a mile. She was, to use the White Sox's announcer's words, the classic low ball hitter. So what did Keyboard do? That's right, fed her one off her shoe tops, a pitch she quickly smacked high off the left field wall for a double, Jefferson scoring. Mudd flied out and so did the Poisons' second baseman, the girl with the green hair, whose nickname was Socks, probably because of the baggy sweat socks she wore outside her pants. Two out, runner at second. We were almost out of the inning — or were we?

No, we weren't. The kid filling in for Bull was a little pip-squeak, even smaller than AD and myself. Like Olive, he batted in an exaggerated crouch, a good bet to walk, and walk he did. "Ball four!" Wart hollered disgustedly, firing the ball back to the pitcher.

"Come on, Keyboard! Bear down!"

Freedburg, up again, hit one out of Olive's reach for a single, and when Ruff hit a single of his own the game was tied, 5–5. We were lucky when Ruff was out trying to steal second, ending the inning.

And that's how it went.

After two innings the score was 7–7, after three, 10–10. We'd take the lead, they'd tie it up, the hits all coming in bunches. Wart shocked us by hitting a home run, a high fly ball that just cleared the left field drainpipe. Keyboard hit one of the hardest balls I'd ever seen (he did it again a few innings later) to center field, knocking over a pile of lawn chairs, a triple all the way. AD doubled twice. I got another hit, a single. So did Olive, who also made two good plays in the field. "Way to go!" I yelled encouragingly. She grinned and, without looking, tipped her cap. Slam walked almost every time up.

Only Ping, Keyboard's brother, went without a hit. But that was okay. We needed him out in left, mostly to run down the balls hit over my head, out by the tot-yard. I left Keyboard in to pitch, even though he'd given up ten runs. What other choice did I have?

The fourth inning was a whopper. Olive opened our half with a walk. I struck out trying to bunt her over to second, much to the delight of Jefferson, who let out a loud "Another sucker gone!" which he gave to everyone who struck out, sometimes, weird as it may seem, to his own teammates. My hand was really starting to hurt. I needed some ice bad, but I wasn't about to leave in the middle of the game.

AD was up. On a 2–0 count, he hit a bouncer over the pitcher's head that neither Freedburg nor Socks could catch. The ball skidded past them toward the outfield, as Olive rounded second and headed for third. She would've made it easily except that the ball hit the curb behind second base and shot straight up in the air, into the glove of a startled Freedburg. He turned and fired to Mudd covering. It was a close play, but Olive was out. "Out!" Jefferson, catcher-umpire, screamed. Olive, who'd slid headfirst, her trademark, picked herself up out of the dirt, a bewildered look on her face. How, she was wondering, had the ball gotten to third so quickly? The dreaded curb had done us in again.

AD, taking second on the throw, moved to third on a Keyboard single, then stayed there as Slam beat out a slow roller back to the pitcher. Bases loaded, two out, Ping up, a perfect time to break out of his . . . er . . . slump. Then again, he was only nine, didn't really like baseball all that much, and was doing us a favor by playing. Too bad he had to be up at such a crucial moment. "Come on, Ping. You can do it!"

The Poisons had a conference on the mound. They decided to change pitchers, bringing in Freedburg from short, moving Mudd to left and the pip-squeak kid in to cover short. Ping, the size and shape of a fire hydrant, stepped to the plate. He batted like he was afraid, with his foot in the bucket. No matter. Freedburg's first pitch, a fast ball, hit him on one bounce in the knee. "Nice pitch!" Keyboard yelled sarcastically. "Cost you a run!"

That it did. AD scampered home. The Roaders had the lead once again, 11–10, bases still loaded, Wart up, followed by Olive.

"Another homer, Wart!" We were all urging him on. Likewise, the Poisons were trying to give Freedburg's confidence a charge. "Fire it, baby! No hitter!" But it was no use. Wart walked on a 3–2 count, forcing in another run. Olive walked. I walked, a good thing, because I could barely grip the bat with my hurt hand. Roaders, 14–10. The Poisons had another conference. "Let 'em hit it, will you?" I heard Jefferson complain. "We'll beat these . . . pansies."

It was AD's turn again. On Freedburg's first pitch he hit a chopper down the third base line for an infield single and another run, but the best — or worst — was about to happen. With three on base, Keyboard, our number three hitter, took a strike down the middle. He swung at the second pitch and missed. "Strike two!" Jefferson screamed. "One more, Freedburg! Way to fire!"

Freedburg wound up, checked the runner at third, and threw. Keyboard swung. THWANG! The tennis ball and the bat collided. WHOOSH! The ball took off like a spark from a Roman candle, as hard hit as his last line drive, the one that knocked down all the lawn chairs. The ball shot out toward left, the runners around the bases. And then, suddenly, there was a sickening sound, one we all knew well. SMASH! The ball had shattered a window, a small one, the ten dollar kind, but still a window.

"Run!" someone shouted. "Let's get out of here!"

Run I did. I grabbed my glove and bat and headed just as fast as I could in the opposite direction, down along the highway, toward home. All around me, kids were running every which way, the kids on our team that is. Our deal with the Poisons, a fair one, went like this: break a window on our field, we pay; break one on yours, you pay. The visiting team didn't wait around for the authorities — neighbors, police, angry parents — to arrive. The home team did. In all the time I'd been playing sandlot ball for the Roaders, I'd chipped in for maybe a half-dozen broken windows, some expensive. The other part of the deal was to finish the game, that afternoon, if possible, on the other team's field. It made sense. Who would've let us play on Hemlock Street after what had just happened? No one, not for a couple of weeks at least, until the window was fixed and paid for.

I spoke to Freedburg on the phone a half-hour later. "We'll be over about one o'clock," he said. "Keyboard gets a ground rule double."

"Runners on second and third," I said. "Two outs, top of the fourth. We lead, let's see . . . 17–10."

"That won't last," he said. There was a funny know-it-all sound in his voice.

"See you this afternoon."

13
Ice in a
Mixing Bowl

It was close to lunch time when AD and I turned off the highway and went up the street toward his house. He'd told me his parents wouldn't be home, and they weren't. I needed to put my swollen right hand in a bucket of ice, but if I tried doing that at my house someone might notice and keep me from playing in the game that afternoon.

AD couldn't find a bucket. Instead, from under the sink, he dug out an enormous mixing bowl, filled it with ice from the freezer, and covered the ice with water. I dunked the hand and kept it under for as long as I could. The icy water made it ache even worse, but I knew that stopping the swelling was my only hope. By now I could barely move my fingers. The knuckles were puffy, sore, and bruised the size and color of rotten peach pits, a dark purple.

I kept the hand under, pulled it out when the cold became too much, waited for the stinging to go away, dunked it back in, pulled it out, in, out, in, out — you get the picture. I figured if I kept the treatment up for an hour or so the swelling might go down and the fingers would loosen enough for me to be able to swing the bat.

After I spoke to Freedburg on the phone to set things up, AD called the other Roaders to make sure they'd be playing. Slam and Wart were ready. So was Olive. Keyboard, figuring the game would be on for the afternoon, had rescheduled his piano lesson for a couple of hours later than usual. Ping would be there too.

"Good thing it's not next Saturday afternoon," AD told me. "I'm playing in a chess tournament. How about some lunch?"

"You're making it?" That sounded dangerous.

"Sure," he said. "Whaddaya want?"

"A pizza, sausage and mushrooms. Extra cheese."

He squinted at me through his glasses. He'd taken the Band-Aid off his nose, showing what was left of the cut he'd gotten running into the tree. I was slumped at the kitchen table, my teeth clenched, holding my hand in the water. "You look pathetic," he said to me. "One step out of a hospital ward. But because I'm such a nice guy I'll make you an AD special: tuna fish with pickles, or grilled cheese, take your pick."

"Tuna fish. Not too much mayo. No pickles."

"We're out of mayonnaise," he said, rummaging through the refrigerator. "How about butter?"

"Tuna fish with butter?" I made a face.

"Take it or leave it."

"Make mine grilled cheese."

He rummaged around some more, pulled out a few ingredients, and went to work. "We've got tomato. Want that, too? Milk?"

"We're up, 17–10," I said, my mind on other things. "Think that's enough?"

"With Keyboard pitching?"

I saw his point.

"No," I said after a moment, "I guess not. One thing's in our favor. We're on our home field, not that closet next door. It's harder to score."

"Oh, if I know the Poisons," said AD, his back to me, "they'll find a way." He was turning up the flame under the frying pan.

"I like your confidence," I said.

We ate our grilled cheese and tomato sandwiches, a whole bag of potato chips, ginger ale (not milk), and some doughnuts, the small kind with powdered sugar on top. When lunch was over and I decided my hand had been in enough ice water for one day, we went outside and sat on the front steps.

"Don't say anything about the hand," I told him. "The fewer people who know about it the better."

"It looks like something out of a horror movie," he said. "How's it feel?"

"Better," I lied. If anything, it felt worse, like a piece of wood attached to the end of my arm. I was holding it away from my body so I wouldn't accidentally rub it against anything. It was too sore to touch.

"Sure it does," said AD, not about to be fooled.

"By the way," I said, changing the subject, "what was so funny about me fighting?"

The memory brought a smile to his face.

"Combination of things," he said. "Your size, for one. Small. It'd be the same if I was fighting. Then there's the way you fight, which is kind of hard to describe; but did you ever see an ant try to take down a Japanese beetle? Or a cat that's gone crazy with catnip?"

"I get the picture," I said, making a disgusted face.

"Mostly it's your role, your personality," he said. "You usually play the peacemaker. We're not used to seeing you kicking and clawing in the dirt. It would've been great to get on film."

"You're a true friend," I said.

"Olive was impressed." His smile flattened into a smirk. His eyes lit up, and then, just like that, they darkened. "What're you going to do about the diving contest?"

"Oh, that." I shrugged. There was only one thing to do — go through with it. Either that or never again swim at the Aquacenter, and be called "chicken pee-wee" for the rest of my life.

"Tell me again what happens when you get up there on the board."

"You saw what happens."

"No, I mean the . . . feeling."

I told him. "Can't breathe. Body goes numb. Itchy. The world spins around. Water so far away, like I'm about to fall off a ten-story building. Everybody watching, me all alone. That's the problem — being stared at." Just thinking about it made me shudder and close my eyes.

"Doubt it," he said.

"I should know," I said indignantly.

"Shooter, you get stared at every day. Up at bat, when

you make a play in the field. Those Little League games with all the parents watching. In class at school. Even at the Aquacenter, diving off the low board. How's that different?"

I thought for a moment. "I . . . er . . . don't know."

"Bet you anything," AD said, "that it's not being watched that's the problem, but the height. I think the word's . . . acrophobia. That's it: fear of heights."

I shook my head and tried to bend my sore fingers, but it was no use. They were as stiff as a stale doughnut.

"What about all the time we spent climbing trees?" I said skeptically. "Or on the roof at school? Your porch roof? Looking out my bedroom window? The escalators at The Plaza, and about a million buildings over one story? Acrobatphobia, no way."

AD laughed at my mistake. "*Acro*phobia," he said. "And you're right, but let's give it a test anyway."

"A test?"

"Follow me."

He took me up to his bedroom on the second floor, a room I'd been in about a zillion times. It was the exact opposite of my room at home: clean and neat as an operating room. There were books all over the room, all put away carefully on shelves. On a table next to his bed was a copy of *The Baseball Encyclopedia* and a couple of computer magazines. AD had his own computer. Lucky him!

We went to the window.

"Look outside!" he commanded.

I did, and I saw a familiar scene: a bunch of trees and

the backs of the houses on the next block. There was a
rusty swing set in AD's back yard, a picnic table with a
portable barbecue at one end, and a lawn mower.

"Like I told you," I said. "No problem."

All at once he threw open the window. A hot breeze
blew in.

"Anything?" he asked.

I shook my head, no.

"Stand closer to the window and look straight down."

"Like I told . . ."

BONG! Without warning, the ground shot down-
ward, fast, and kept on moving, farther and farther away,
ten stories, twenty, instead of two. What's worse, the
ground, the yard, and everything began to spin. It was
like being on a cosmic merry-go-round, looking at the
world through the wrong end of a telescope. A beach
ball that'd been lying by AD's back door had — like
that! — become a colored grapefruit, a marble, a dot;
the picnic table became a tray, then a brown baseball
card. I froze. My body itched all over. A huge vise
grabbed my chest and started to squeeze. "Uh . . . uh . . .
uh . . ." I was too scared to speak or even shut my eyes.
My head pitched forward, out the window. I was a
goner.

"Whoa there!"

It was AD, grabbing hold of me at the last instant and
pulling me back inside.

"Look straight ahead!" he commanded.

I did, and — like that! — the world stopped moving.
There were the trees, the backs of the neighbors' houses,

the swing set and lawn mower. My legs stopped wobbling, my heart slowed down to a trot. I could breathe
again.

"AD," I sputtered, "I almost fainted! The ground . . .
everything spinning, far away. Awful."

"Look down again," he told me. "Slowly."

"No, I . . ."

"I've got a hold of you," he said reassuringly. "Do it!"

I took a peek. There it was again, the merry-go-round
world, my breath out of me in a rush. This time I shut
my eyes. AD pulled me away.

"Acrophobia," he said. "You've got it bad."

What an understatement!

"Let's try one more experiment," he said.

"No!"

He ignored me and shut the window with a bang.

"Now look," he said.

I did cautiously, my cheek pressed against the glass.
The picnic table stayed a table, the beach ball a beach
ball. A cat ran along the side of the house, just in sight.
The yard wobbled, but only a little.

"I don't get it," I said, puzzled as could be.

"You're afraid of falling," he said. "It's that simple."

"But what about all those other times I've been up in
the air? The trees, the porch roofs?"

He shrugged. "That was then. This is now. It explains
your problem on the diving board. Way up there, all by
yourself, no pane of glass to protect you from —"

"From crashing. From flattening myself. Bruises and
broken bones."

AD nodded. "Afraid so," he said.

"What do I do now?"

"Skip the diving contest and tell your parents."

At the moment I was too confused to do either.

14
Game Two, Part Two

Surprise, surprise! Bull Reilly was back from the dentist and ready to play. The sight of him, in his dungarees and greasy sweat shirt, just about knocked me flat. No wonder Freedburg had sounded so funny on the phone. He'd known about it all along, as I should have. After all, how long did a dentist appointment take?

The game began right away. We had a short argument about the score (the Poisons claimed we had only fifteen runs, not seventeen), but when Freedburg told his own teammates they were wrong the argument ended. Keyboard took his place on second, AD on third, two outs, Slam the batter. Except that instead of facing a wild Freedburg on the mound, there stood Bull, already soaking with sweat, his huge fist crushing the ball, which looked as shrunken as a white acorn.

"Play ball!" Jefferson hollered.

Slam struck out on three pitches.

Now that it was the Roaders' turn to take the field, I made a change. I knew better than anyone that my sore hand would make it hard for me to throw as well as bat, so I switched positions with Slam, moving him to short-stop, me to first, where I'd mostly have to catch. "What for?" Slam asked, as surprised as the others, all except AD.

"You're the better shortstop," Keyboard said.

"Never mind," I told the rest of them. "I know what I'm doing."

There were some good reasons why I didn't want anybody other than AD to know that I was hurt. I'd been hurt only eight or ten times in my whole life. That isn't bad considering all the sports and horsing around I did, like going up and down the escalators the wrong way in The Plaza's big department store, bicycle jumping, run-sheep-run, BB gun wars, things like that — or things I used to do all the time when I was younger. I'd broken my wrist once when a dog had chased me and I'd fallen in the street. I'd sprained my ankle, chipped a tooth, dislocated my left big toe, gotten a minor concussion running into my basement wall, been stung by bees and stitched up a few times, but that was all. Nothing much out of the ordinary. Nothing that any of the other kids on our team, or the Poisons, hadn't done. Some had done worse. Like Wart, who'd broken his leg playing football. He had to wear a cast all winter and spring and missed half of the baseball season. And Keyboard, who'd hurt his back once and was in, I think it's called, traction. At the hospital, too. Games, as you might expect, had had all kinds of broken bones, cuts and bruises. So had Freedburg, who in kindergarten had taken a nose-dive off the school roof.

No matter, I liked to keep my injuries to myself. I didn't want anyone making excuses for me, or telling me what to do — like not play baseball — or interfering with my plans. I hated to have anybody feeling sorry for me. I was used to solving my own problems, most of them anyway. Maybe that's why, after finding out about Olive's brother, I decided to back off, not try to force him to do something he didn't want to do. Whether he played baseball for the Roaders or not was up to him.

Keyboard finished his warm-ups. No one on either team could remember who had made the last out for the Poisons in their half of the third inning, so they started over, at the top of their order. Bull, the newcomer, was to bat last. The Poisons still had seven players, even adding Bull, because Mickey Mudd hadn't been able to make it. His father'd heard about the broken window and had grounded him.

Freedburg, pulling the ball as usual, lined one down the left field line, all the way to Gertie Gershwin's drainpipe, his long black hair flying as he scrambled into second base with a double. Ruff grounded to Olive, moving Freedburg to third. Jefferson followed by hitting a high fly ball beyond second, which AD would've caught racing in from center ("I got it! I got it!") if he hadn't crashed into Olive, who'd gotten in his way. The ball hit the ground untouched. The run scored. Jefferson ended up on third, still with only one out. Make that two when Big Foot whipped her bat around at a high pitch and popped out to Wart.

"You got 'em, Keyboard! One more! Let's hear some chatter!"

Socks surprised us. She was a skinny waif, a miniature Olive, but she lined one of Keyboard's fast balls over my head and into the ten-foot-high bush in short right for a run-scoring double. Out of breath, she stood on second, pulling up her baggy socks, even though it was about one hundred degrees outside. The rest of the Poisons gave her a raucous cheer. Olive glided over and started talking to her. The two of them were squeaking like a couple of baby pigs when the pip-squeak kid came to the plate and ended the inning by grounding out. We held the lead, 17–12.

As usual, Bull was his overpowering self on the mound, striking out the side in the fifth and sixth, to the total delight of Tom Jefferson ("Strike three, sucker!") and the rest of the Poisons. Only AD managed to reach base for us, getting a cheap hit up the first base line by beating the throw to first. He then stole second and third, but died there when both Keyboard and Slam fanned. I was as useless as a broken record and probably should've taken myself out of the game. I couldn't grip the bat hard enough to swing with any power, and my bunt attempts all failed, but I kept telling myself that the team needed me to field, which I did. Hang in there, Shooter!

Keyboard was doing better than expected, until the seventh. Bull, a giant swinging a toothpick at the plate, led off by walking. He trotted down to first, where I tried to hold him close to the bag. He stank, no two ways about it. Probably it was all that sweat pouring out from beneath the brim of his hat, soaking his bulging neck and face and shirt. He leaned over, hands on his knees, and kept a close eye on Keyboard. Bent over, Bull was still taller than I was, a real monster. The side of his face showed the shadow of a beard. How old was this guy, anyway?

On Keyboard's first pitch to Freedburg, Bull stole second, standing. Wart had dropped the ball behind the plate and hadn't even gotten off a throw. Keyboard turned his back to the plate and glared angrily out to center field, muttering under his breath, no doubt one of his patented swears.

"Wake up, Wart!" I shouted.

On the very next pitch Bull stole third. No one, meaning Slam, had covered. Mistakes came from tension. No one was talking it up. We were playing like we were behind instead of ahead by five runs. As coach, it was up to me to do something.

"Time!" I called out.

Infield, catcher, and pitcher huddled on the mound.

"Come on," I said. "Concentrate. A five-run lead is nothing for these guys to make up. Let's not let 'em back in the game. Let's hear some chatter!"

"Right!" Wart shouted. We broke the huddle.

"Let's go, Keyboard! No batter! No batter!"

Keyboard did his best, but, after all, he was an outfielder, not a pitcher. He got Freedburg to pop up, Bull holding third, got Ruff to hit a grounder, an easy bouncer to me at first. I fielded it cleanly and was about to run over and step on first for the second out when I saw Bull take off for home. Forgetting about my bad hand, I wheeled and fired. The ball wobbled in the air and landed halfway between first and home. Bull scored easily.

Forget Bull. Pain shot up and down my arm. I

dropped my glove, grabbing hold of my bad hand with my good one. The fingers were hot and throbbing. My eyes filled with tears.

"What's wrong, Shooter?" Keyboard ran over from the mound looking worried. Wart and Slam and Olive headed in my direction, too, but I stood up and, with my good hand, waved them all away. "It's nothing. Just a . . . sore hand. It'll be all right."

"You're sure?" Keyboard gave me a skeptical look.

I nodded, not at all sure. But I picked up my glove and put it back on. The Poisons were watching me closely. Any sign of weakness and watch out! They'd be all over me like sharks after red meat. Once we had a kid, name of Westerhausen — we called him "Beer" for short — who was the worst fielder in the world. The only thing to do was to stick him out in right field where, we figured, he couldn't get in any trouble. We figured wrong. As soon as the Poisons caught on to his problem (Beer could catch about as well as a telephone pole), they tried to hit every pitch to right, to make Beer do the fielding. Poor kid. After a couple of games, which we lost, we moved him in to second, where the shortstop and first baseman could protect him. He quit playing about halfway through the summer.

Just as I suspected, the very next batter, Jefferson, bunted one up the first base line. I ran in to field the ball, which I did, but when I tried to throw it to Keyboard, who was covering first, I couldn't. The thought of pain shooting up and down my arm made me hang onto the ball. Jefferson was safe at first and Ruff moved all the way to third. The Poisons loved it.

"Nice play, kid! Way to throw it!"

Jefferson had a big grin on his face. The only good thing was that he also had a sore-looking red welt on his forehead, where my knuckles had struck home.

"If they bunt again," Keyboard told me, "I'll field the ball, you cover first."

A good strategy but the Poisons had to test it. Big Foot, next up, copied Jefferson, bunting down the first base line. Only it was Wart, not Keyboard, jumping out from catcher's position (ever see a rhino jump?), who scooped up the ball and winged it to me for the second out. Ruff scored on the play, Jefferson took second, then raced home a moment later on another double by Socks, her second into the bush in right. And when the pip-squeak singled it was 17–16, a crummy one-run lead, with Bull coming to the plate.

"Walk him intentionally," was my advice to Keyboard. He did, and the strategy worked. Freedburg, next up, flied out to end the inning.

"Strike one! Two! Out, sucker!" Jefferson whooped behind the plate, as our first hitter, Wart, went down swinging. "Strike one! Two! Out!" he whooped again, when Olive did the same. My turn up. Me, with my horrible hand and the lightest bat I could find. Not that the bat mattered. Bull threw too hard. Even at the best of times I didn't do well against him, but when I could barely grip the bat? Forget it. "Strike one! Two! Out, sucker!"

15
The Cinderella Kid

The Poisons' half of the eighth inning was short and . . . a killer. Ruff smashed one over AD's head in center, a ball that rolled and rolled and kept on rolling until Ruff had an inside-the-park home run to tie the game. "Way to go, Ruffian!" The Poisons' bench went berserk. "One more run! One more run!"

They didn't have to wait long. After a Slam error, Big Foot golfed a low inside fast ball onto Gertie's roof for the second home run of the inning, a 19–17 Poisons' lead, and it didn't seem to matter that Keyboard (where, oh where was Games!) bore down and got the next three batters out to end the inning. It was now the ninth, three outs to go, and we were losing — again.

We ran off the field with our heads down, only to find the new kid standing by himself, leaning against a tree behind home plate. In all the excitement I hadn't even seen him crossing the field.

"Well if it isn't The Cinderella Kid," AD said to me under his breath. "Better late than never. You going to ask him to play?"

I shook my head. "No way. He should've been here earlier. Besides, we don't need him." But secretly I was glad he'd come.

"That's the spirit," AD said, giving me a wink.

"What's the score?" The Kid asked his sister. Olive's pink tongue stuck out of her mouth. She looked nervous. "We're down by two," she said.

That we were.

AD was a tough hitter. He had a good eye, despite being what I'd call blind, and hardly ever swung at a bad pitch. Bull fired two quick strikes past him, then three balls, two in the dirt, the other way outside. After each pitch, Jefferson tossed the tennis ball back to him from his catcher's crouch, trying to look as cool and unconcerned as he could. He took his time flashing Bull the next sign, no doubt another fast ball. AD, waiting, tapped his bat on the plate. Bull spit once in the dirt, wound up, and blazed one. The ball sailed about a foot over AD's head. Ball four. AD headed for first.

"Strike three!" Jefferson screamed. "You're out!"

"WHAT! Come off it, Jefferson! Fungofandanglefat, you creep!"

We were all set to argue, no one more angrily than AD, when Bull cut us short. He hardly ever spoke, but when he did you listened. His voice was a match for his size, rumbling, like a volcano erupting.

"Ball four," was all he said.

He was fierce, but fair. He didn't need to cheat to win, and he knew it.

With one out, Slam beat out an infield roller, moving AD to second. Ping was next up. "Don't try to kill it,"

I told him. "Just meet the ball. Get those runners into scoring position."

Ping shut his eyes and swung as hard as he could, pretty hard for somebody's younger brother, and — "Way to go, Ping!" — lined one up the middle for a hit. Ruff charged in from center, tried fielding the ball on the dead run like he was supposed to, in order to keep AD from scoring, but missed it clean. At the last instant the ball took a bad bounce and went on by him. SCREECH! He put the brakes on and ran the ball down as AD scored and Slam, rounding third, headed for home with the tying run.

Ruff hit Freedburg, the cut-off man, behind second base. Freedburg pegged the ball home. Slam was . . . out.

"Zapashucamarmalade!"

We all let out a noisy groan. Now there were two outs and we were still down a run, Ping at second; our weakest hitter, if you didn't count me and my hurt hand, was coming up.

I should've had more faith, that's for sure. Wart, looking great for a blob of beef, got what must've been his first hit ever off Bull, a pop single to left, Ping taking third. We were still alive.

"WHOOP-DE! Way to go, Wartsky!"

I practically swallowed my gum, then held my breath as Olive, crouching lower than ever, walked. Bull pounded the ball in his glove, disgusted.

"Come on, Shooter! A hit's a run. A single, a walk. Anything!"

A terrible feeling, the kind you have watching a centipede crawl out of your lunch bag, suddenly made

me squirm. Those shouts were for the next batter —
me. Oh, no!

I knew it'd come to this. I should've taken myself out
of the game long ago. I'd been lousy in the field and at
the plate. My hand looked like an elephant had stepped
on it. The thing had no feeling. Something was probably broken inside. But could I back out now, even if it
was for the good of the team?

"Time!"

I had a brilliant idea.

"Hey, John," I said to The Cinderella Kid. "Hit for
me."

"Who?" he said, startled. His mouth flapped open.
"Me?"

"Yeah. Who else's named John around here?" I went
over to him. "See this?" I asked him. In order to hold up
my hurt hand, I had to lift it with my good one.

"It looks broken," he mumbled.

"I can't swing the bat," I said. "You can."

"I don't know . . ." he mumbled again. His eyeballs
were like olives in a jar of vinegar, bobbing about every
which way.

"Let's go!" Jefferson shouted. "I wanna go swimming!"

"Whaddaya say?" I asked The Kid.

"Okay," he said, just like that. He stood up straight
and wiped his mouth with the back of his hand, went
over and picked up a bat, the longest broom handle we
had, and stood at the plate, tall as could be, feet wide
apart, bat pointing skyward. I was so excited my heart
was a pounding fist inside my chest.

"Strike one!"

The first pitch sizzled past The Kid before he moved. It was clear as the sweat on his face that Bull wasn't nearly as impressed with the newcomer as the rest of us. For him, as always, it was the competition, the more the better. The new kid was a fresh face, new blood. The Kid's size (he was at least as tall as Bull) was scary and so were his muscular arms, but Bull wasn't backing down an inch. Besides, with the bases loaded, the game was on the line.

"Come on, John!" Olive squeaked from first.

The rest of us were weirdly silent. So were the Poisons, all except Jefferson.

"Strike two!"

The fast ball slammed into Jefferson's mitt.

"Come on, John! Swing! You can do it!"

He could, no question. On the next pitch, a sizzler like the others, The Kid's bat gave a nervous wiggle, a twitch, and he swung. THWONK! The ball took off like a charge of dynamite, clearing Gertie's roof by about twenty feet and disappearing beyond.

"Foul ball!" Jefferson bellowed. Unfortunately it was. But what a blast! And The Kid'd gotten around on it. Never in my life had I known anyone strong enough to pull a Bull fast ball, until The Cinderella Kid, that is.

"Straighten it out, Kid!"

The next pitch, low and outside, was a ball. So was the next. The heat and tension were fierce, worse than ever. No one spoke. No one moved, except Bull. The runners on base didn't even take their leads. Everyone was watching The Kid, who looked solid as a boulder, bat cocked, ready. Bull was ready, too. He wound up, kicked his leg out, and threw as hard as he could.

Hard as he could was how The Kid swung, too, with a wiggle of the bat and a vicious cut that sucked in all the air around home plate. And the ball, where did it go? Straight up, that's where, a major league pop-up if ever there was one. AD, off with the crack — I mean thwonk — of the bat, scampered home. The ball hung, suspended in midair, then plummeted. The Poisons, our bench, The Kid, all of us stood mesmerized. The ball was going to fall in! No one was going to catch it! We were going to tie the game up — maybe win! Run, Kid!

Down it came — straight into Bull's bare hand. He hadn't even bothered to use his glove. He smiled toothily. The game was over.

16
Plans in the Works

"How would you boys like to put on an exhibition game?" Mr. Sparkle asked, from behind the counter inside his candy store. AD, Slam, and Wart had met me out front. They still had their bathing suits on from swimming at the Aquacenter. I was back from the doctor's where, much to my relief, I'd learned that my hand was definitely not broken. The x-rays proved it. As protection, the doctor had put my arm in a sling. "How'd you hurt it?" my father had asked me on the way to the doctor's. "Baseball," I'd muttered. He wouldn't like to hear that I'd been in a fight.

Mr. Sparkle's question surprised us.

"Exhibition? You mean a baseball game?"

"Pony League style," said Mr. Sparkle.

"Where would we play? When —"

"Come on out back and I'll tell you all about it."

The back of the store was a cluttered storage room, mostly full of boxes and equipment, books, magazines, junk. A desk with a messy top was up against one wall.

A radio was playing music, the classical kind AD and Keyboard's parents were always listening to. An air conditioner blew cool air around the room. We sat on some folding chairs and the desk, all except Wart, who sat on the floor. He was chewing on a piece of black licorice. All of us were eating something. Mr. Sparkle slurped a grape Sno-Kone.

"I had a long talk with the Village Council this week," he began. "And the Recreation Department. They're all agreed. A Pony League is definitely in order. They've been thinking about organizing one for quite a while, but for one reason or another something always got in the way. There's supposed to be a town meeting in two weeks, and I think we can get them to vote on it if —" He stopped talking.

"If what, Mr. Sparkle?" AD asked.

"Well," Mr. Sparkle said, "there has to be some interest shown. It's important to get a lot of parents and kids — Pony League–age kids, your age, junior high school — to come to the town meeting that night and show support. Also some local merchants, sponsors to offer to pay for the uniforms, like myself. The village would pay for the rest. That ought to do it. There's no reason not to have a Pony League, and it's high time Edgewater Township did. Only I was thinking, wouldn't it be fun to stage a one-game exhibition a few days before the meeting, invite the village councilors, the merchants, your parents, friends, anybody interested? Show them what good baseball players we've got in this town . . . you are good, aren't you?"

We looked around at each other. Mr. Sparkle was smiling, kidding.

"All except Shooter here," said AD.

I threw an M&M at him with my left hand.

"I was noticing your hand, Shooter," Mr. Sparkle said. "Nice color. Sort of like my Sno-Kone. Have you had it looked at?"

I nodded. "It's just badly bruised," I told him, like I'd told the others outside. "I can play again when it feels better. A week to ten days the doctor said. Maybe a little longer."

"The game would have to be a week from next Saturday," Mr. Sparkle said. "I hope that gives you enough time. Questions? Suggestions?"

Wart raised his hand. The rest of us gave him a dirty look. Where did he think he was, anyway? School?

"Er . . . I'm not s-sure who's playing," he said.

"You are," Mr. Sparkle said. "Against the team you always play against." The front doorbell jingled — some customer — and Mr. Sparkle got up. "Do you think they'd be interested?"

"The Poisons? I'm afraid they would," I answered.

"Wait here," said Mr. Sparkle, looking puzzled. "I'll be right back."

By the time we left the candy store, Mr. Sparkle had filled us in on all the details. An exhibition game involving the whole village would take a lot of planning and work ahead of time. All the players would have to be notified, the usual ones, McCarthy Roaders and Hemlock Street Poisons, as well as a few extras. "If the game's going to mean something," Mr. Sparkle said, "then we need nine to a side." The players' parents would be sent invitations to the game and asked to sign an insurance form, in case somebody — me, for instance — got hurt. The Edgewater Township village councilors would also be sent invitations, as would all the local merchants, potential sponsors. "I pretty much know the ones who'll come," Mr. Sparkle told us. "And I'll talk to them personally."

He said he was also going to recruit some of our parents and some of the local village club leaders, like, I think he called it, the ladies' auxiliary, to help out with the arrangements. He'd get someone to be in charge of invitations, insurance forms, refreshments (there was going to be a refreshment stand at the field!), and someone to write an ad announcing the game in the local paper. The Recreation Department had already told him it would get the field in shape, supply the bases and plate and pitching rubber. What about the balls and bats? "Don't worry about that," Mr. Sparkle said. "I'm sure the local sports shop will be happy to donate them for a worthy cause."

"What about umpires?"

"I'll call balls and strikes," said Mr. Sparkle. "Maybe the Rec can help with an umpire on the bases. And I'll order some shirts and hats and batting helmets, a different color for each team, with 'Sparkle's Candy Shack' written on the back."

It was clear that Mr. Sparkle was behind us all the way. AD told me he'd heard that Mr. Sparkle used to be a school teacher. Maybe one reason he owned a candy store was so he could still be around kids. It made sense to me.

Three days later an ad appeared in the newspaper.

Town Picnic

Exhibition Baseball Game

The Edgewater Township Ladies' Auxiliary, in conjunction with the Village Recreation Department and Sparkle's Candy Shack, announces its first annual town picnic and jamboree, to be held at Indianwood Field, Saturday, August 16, 12:00 noon to 4:00 P.M. Food, drinks, rides, music, contests. Talk to neighbors, win a prize, get stuffed, have a good time. Exhibition baseball game played by McCarthy Roaders vs. Hemlock Street Poisons, 2:00 P.M. Rain date, August 23. All are invited.

The response to the ad was "outstanding," to use Mr. Sparkle's word. We stopped by his store a few days after the ad came out.

"Outstanding," he kept saying. "My phone hasn't stopped ringing."

It seemed that there were quite a few villagers who thought that a get-together and a picnic were just the right thing, even in August, when you'd figure a lot of people would be away on vacation.

"Some are," Mr. Sparkle told us. "Some aren't. You've been to the Aquacenter. Look how crowded it is. The Village Council has been informed and they're all set, most of them. Enough. I've got a handful of local merchants committed to sponsoring a team next year. They'll contact the Rec when the time comes. Shooter, your mom, in case she hasn't told you, is in charge of the refreshment stand during the game —"

"Mine, too," Slam said. "Shooter's mom called her."

"Good," said Mr. Sparkle, giving his hands a clap. He was as excited as the rest of us. Well, maybe not that much. After all, we were the ones playing in the game. And my hand, although it was still in its sling, was getting better by the day.

It turned out that almost all the local clubs and organizations, even the Boy Scouts, were making food for the picnic and getting the picnic tables in order. There would be rides for the little kids — a couple of ponies, a merry-go-round, a miniature Ferris wheel loaned to the village by The Heights, a neighboring town. The fire department was putting on some sort of demonstration, which they were keeping a secret, the junior high school band would perform, and the newspaper was covering the event, including the baseball game.

"Are all the players set?" Mr. Sparkle asked me.

"I think so. The Poisons'll all be there. No doubt about it. They even picked up three extra players who don't usually play, but who wanted to be in the exhibition. They're not the greatest players, but the rest of the Poisons'll make up for them, you can bet."

"How about your team?"

"It's coming," AD said. "Keyboard was supposed to go away on vacation with his parents, but they're leaving a day later so he can play. All of us here are set. Our starting pitcher looks doubtful, but you never know.

He's in trouble with his mother and we haven't talked to him in a while. Olive, one of our other players, can play. We think her brother can, too. He's kind of . . . strange." He shrugged and looked over at me.

"We picked up a couple of extra ones, too," I added. "They're not exactly what we need, but we'll practice with them this week."

"Show 'em a few of the finer points," Mr. Sparkle said with a mock smile.

"Right. And Olive said she had somebody else, just in case. She wouldn't tell me who. She's a little strange, too."

AD snickered. So did Slam and Wart.

"How about a Sno-Kone?" said Mr. Sparkle. "On the house."

Who could turn that down?

"There's one more thing, Mr. Sparkle," AD said. "Not all the players are Pony League age. Olive isn't. Wart here. One or two of our new kids. A couple of the Poisons either. Next summer many of them'll be in their last year of Little League. Isn't this supposed to be a Pony League exhibition?"

"No problem," Mr. Sparkle said. "As long as most of you are old enough, and the baseball's good."

"Oh, it'll be good, all right," I said. "Just you wait."

"Outstanding!"

The phone was ringing when we left.

17
Hole in One
for a Cheeseburger

AD didn't win the chess tournament he played in. He was captain of the chess club at school and won plenty of tournaments, but not this one, a summer state-wide event held in Chicago. "Not even close," he told the rest of us. Knowing AD, more than likely the tournament was *very* close; a pawn here or a bishop there would've meant first prize. It wasn't AD's style to brag, not even when he won. And the things he was good at — mental games like chess, cards, video stuff — he won often. He was also tops at miniature golf, even better than Keyboard, who still sometimes beats him, I think, by sheer will power.

Monday afternoon, five days before the picnic and the biggest game of our lives, the clouds rolled in, the darkest, most ominous ones way off in the distance. The weather, which had been hot as an overworked fuse, suddenly turned cool and breezy, one of those summer days, so said my dad, when you could feel fall in the air.

The only thing I was feeling was the grip of the lawn

mower. My dad, who worked as foreman in a factory, had Mondays off. At breakfast he'd taken a look at my bruised hand, no longer in its protective sling but still a light purple, asked me to make a fist, and when I did, pronounced me fit. I thought he meant fit for Saturday's game, but what he really meant was the lawn.

"Perfect day for it," he said. "You won't even break into a sweat."

We didn't have a whole lot of lawn, half an infield's worth in front, on a sharp rise up from the street, tennis court size in back, same as our neighbors'. Anyone could've easily done the job with a hand mower, but because I mowed lawns every week for a summer job (this year I had ten customers) my dad had bought a secondhand power mower at a yard sale. The thing was always breaking down, but I'd learned to do most of the repairs myself. My dad's hobby was mechanics, and in some ways I took after him.

I'd finished mowing our lawn, front and back, and was starting to work behind our next door neighbor's house, head down, letting the mower do all the work, thinking about my two main problems — how to get Games back on the ball field and the Aquacenter high board diving contest — when I heard some shouting far off, a good block away. But when I looked up, it was Slam and AD standing right next to me, trying to get my attention above the roar and clank of the power mower. I shifted into neutral and let it idle.

"We're going golfing . . . this afternoon . . . wanna come?" They took turns shouting at me, slowly moving their mouths, exaggerating the words.

"Gotta finish!" I shouted back. "Three more lawns to go!" I held up three fingers.

"Not now. This afternoon."

"Count me in."

"What?"

"Count me in!" I threw the gears into forward, and away I went.

"Golfing" meant miniature golf, an easier game to play than real golf, the kind you saw played on TV. Miniature golf was more a game than a sport. It didn't cost very much; you could win a free game if you were lucky; the place — Minigolf it was called — supplied the putters and golf balls; and we always bet against one another for prizes. The prizes were almost always food, mostly because there was a fast-food restaurant, a hamburger hole-in-the-wall, right next door.

Minigolf was a long bike ride from McCarthy Road, three or four miles up the highway, on the border of Edgewater Township and The Heights. We always took the back route, staying clear of the highway and traffic, cutting through The Plaza parking lot, speeding down side streets, through neighborhoods a lot like our own.

Keyboard, who never missed Minigolf if he could help it, AD, Slam, and myself set off around lunch time. We thought of asking The Cinderella Kid if he wanted to join us, but then we probably would've had to ask Olive, and I wasn't ready to put up with all the jokes I'd hear about the two of us. For some reason, beats me, the others had gotten the ridiculous idea that Olive had her eye on me, and worse, that I had mine on her. Like

I said, ridiculous. I talked the others out of asking either of them.

Then there was Games. The only time I'd seen him in a week was when he rode past my house in his mother's car, Sunday morning, probably on their way to church. He flashed his Dracula smile at me, large teeth hanging over his lower lip, eyeballs spinning crazily in their sockets, and I'd waved, but the car didn't stop. Since the day AD and I'd gone over to Games's house and talked to his mother, I'd called him a few times, but without any luck. He couldn't talk and, like his mom told us, he was grounded indefinitely. What had she said? Until he proved he could be trusted — that's it. But how do you prove that?

We — the club that is — had talked over the problem. We needed Games to pitch on Saturday. Without him we were sure losers unless The Cinderella Kid wanted to pitch, and who knew about him. "I'd hate to get out there and make a fool of myself," Keyboard admitted. He knew he wasn't a pitcher. Good hit, no pitch. So getting Games back was crucial, an absolute must. But how? Nobody had an answer, not even AD.

"It's more than just the game," he said, speaking for the rest of us, as he often did. "Times are always more fun when Games's around."

We hated to see a buddy in trouble.

Even though it was a weekday afternoon, the Mini-golf was crowded and we had to wait a while to start. The man who took our money, a skinny guy with a handlebar mustache and a diamond earring, was extra busy but looked pleased that he had so many customers.

He gave us each a putter and a colored ball and told us the wait would be about ten minutes.

"What'll we play for?" Keyboard asked. He was writing down our names on a paper scorecard. "Winner take all?"

"No way," I said. "Give the rest of us a chance."

"How about two prizes?" said AD. "One for the best score. One for most holes in one. Agreed?"

It was agreed.

"But what'll we play for?" Keyboard asked again. He loved competing for prizes, mostly because he won a lot. No matter, win or lose, the rest of us liked it, too.

Waiting, I could feel my lips start to sweat, my stomach squeeze and squish like a sponge, and every now and then rumble about as loud as the thunder off in the distance. My juices were on overdrive. To calm down I did my usual: chomped on a wad of gum.

"A giant milk shake for the winner," AD said. "A cheeseburger for most holes in one."

"Let's have a third prize," I suggested, a brainstorm. "Large fries for the most . . . ridiculous shot. Majority vote."

The others thought about this new wrinkle to the game. They were all smiling, imagining what they could do with a putter and a golf ball.

"Good thing Games isn't here," Keyboard said. "He'd find a way to win that one hands down. Kill some rodent with the ball or something."

We all laughed. Again it was agreed.

Right from the start I was, you might say, like a weather vane in a wind tunnel, winging around the course, holing all my shots, using the incredibly deft touch you needed on the pool-table greens. On the very first hole I made a hole in one, another on the fourth, putting me way ahead of the field. Anyone watching would've thought I was the world's champion miniature golfer. As a matter of fact, there was someone watching. The guy who owned the place, the one with the earring. He made a "go-get-'em" sign with his fist when I looked his way.

"Don't worry," Keyboard told the others, "he'll cool off."

"Oh yeah?" I said smugly. "I can already taste that cheeseburger and shake."

Unbelievably, on the sixth hole, I scored another hole in one, number three. Keyboard also got one, his first, the only other player to do so. For me, there was nothing like a little confidence to make the going easier. Come to think of it, it was the same with baseball. What was missing when we played Bull Reilly and the Poisons was confidence. We took the field against them knowing we were going to lose, and we did.

Minigolf had funny names for all the different holes. The eighth hole, a dogleg to the right with a windmill spinning around in the middle of it, was called "Holland Horror." The ninth, called "Zip Your Lip" ("Why not 'pants'?" Keyboard asked), zigzagged from tee to so-called green. A clown's face with a movable mouth that clamped open and shut while you tried to hit your ball was known as "Clowning Around." Some we'd already played were "Basket Case," "A Bun in the Oven," "Hopscotch," and my favorite, "Volcano Burp," a green felt pyramid that had a hole at the very top. When you missed, which was easy to do, the ball came right back at you and you had to start over. Keyboard called this one "Vomit Belch."

At the end of nine holes, halfway around the course, I led by an unbelievable five strokes. Holes in one: Shooter 3, Keyboard 1. "He'll fade," Keyboard kept saying. AD and Slam were quick to agree. What else could they say?

The tenth hole, "Water Torture," made you hit your ball along a ramp, over a foot-deep pool of slimy water, and onto another ramp, but not so hard that the ball would hit the wooden backstop and roll into the water coming back the other way.

AD, up first, hit it perfectly, just hard enough. So did Slam and myself. Keyboard, last up, really teed off, smashing a bouncer over the water on one gigantic hop. The ball banged the backstop — THUNK! — richocheted back — "No! No!" Keyboard screamed — and, with a splash, landed in the water.

"Twirpitch!"

"Look out!" AD warned. "You want to get us tossed out?"

But the man up front was busy with another customer and wasn't watching.

Usually when your ball ends up in the water you have to start over, but Keyboard's ball was in only halfway. "I'll hit it out," he said confidently. And while the rest of us stood aside, he took a vicious practice swing, like he was all set to clobber one about two hundred yards with a driver, stuck his nose over the edge of the water, which was green with slime, brought the club head back, and really let go. The ball and about twenty gallons of water went shooting up in the air, soaking the rest of us.

"Disgusting!" Slam sputtered.

"Way to go, Keyboard! Jerk!"

He almost fell down laughing.

"You look like a bunch of garbage disposals!" he howled.

"Very funny, fungus face!"

We chased him around the hole, pelting him with gobs of slime. The man running the place stood up and looked in our direction, but by the time he'd finished handing out some more golf balls and putters we'd calmed down enough for him to forget about us. I was anxious to keep playing. The thought of a free lunch made my stomach rumble all the more. Keyboard, no question about it, had won large fries for the most ridiculous shot. The others, wiping off their faces, had to agree.

I held the lead all the way to the seventeenth hole, three strokes over both Keyboard and AD, who'd been steadily gaining on me over the back nine. No matter what I did, I'd won a cheeseburger for being two holes in one ahead of the field with only two holes to go.

The seventeenth hole, called "Fried Eggs," was in the shape of a frying pan, with the tee at the far end of the so-called handle. You were supposed to hit your ball into the middle of the green, er, pan, where a number of yellow swells, I guess they were supposed to be egg yolks, surrounded the hole. Whenever your ball hit one of the swells it would roll in the opposite direction, away from the hole, a costly penalty. Slam, up first, aced it, a hole in one, but he was too far behind on all accounts to catch up. We all gave him a mock cheer. Being the newcomer, he didn't have as much experience at the Minigolf as the rest of us.

Fried Eggs turned out to be my worst hole of the day. No matter what I did, I couldn't seem to get my ball past the swells and into the hole. Keyboard had his own troubles — "Fungofandanglefat!" — and took a seven. So did I. AD, sliding in a five-footer for a four, tied me for first. One hole to go.

Hole number eighteen wasn't what you might expect. It was really the only normal hole on the course, a straight line from tee to hole without any obstructions, tilts, tunnels, zigzags, curves, traps, or distractions. All you needed to do was aim right and hit your ball, exactly what AD did. PING! Off it went, straight for the hole, a sure hole in one, except for one thing: he hadn't hit it hard enough. The ball stopped an inch short.

"Gimme a break!" he hollered.

The rest of us hooted at him. He still had a piece of green slime looped over his ear and another stuck to his forehead. Of course no one told him how stupid he looked.

My turn was next. I stroked the finest ball I'd hit all day, like AD's, straight for the hole. Again there was a problem. AD's ball was in the way. If it hadn't been, I'd have chalked up my fourth hole in one. Instead it knocked AD's ball all the way over against one of the sideboards and landed about a foot away. He missed his shot. I made mine, no problem, winning a giant milk shake and a cheeseburger, payable on the spot. And boy, was I hungry.

Free food, a Minigolf victory — but the best was yet to come.

"Lucky all the way, sucker," Keyboard was saying to me as we handed in our putters and golf balls, but the man who ran the place interrupted him.

"Any of you boys interested in a job?"

"What kind?"

"Maintenance," he said. The diamond in his ear sparkled. It was hard to take your eyes off it. "Yard work, painting, mowing the grass, that sort of thing. Being a handyman."

"You mean here, at the Minigolf?"

The man nodded. He had a friendly smile.

"I could use some help," he said.

The four of us looked at one another.

"I've already got a job mowing lawns," I said.

"Me, too," said AD. "A job that is."

Slam and Keyboard just shrugged. They had summer jobs, too. And Keyboard had piano lessons.

"Guess not," the man said. "Too bad. Pay's pretty good. Flexible hours."

"Sorry," I said.

We started to walk off.

"Wait a minute!" said AD, banging his head with the heel of his hand. The two pieces of slime, now dry as sand, popped off his face and ear. "Hey, mister," he said. "We have a friend who might be interested. When would you need to know?"

"Sooner the better. Today'd be best. I'm in a hurry."

"Today it is," AD said, practically shouting. "Don't give that job away."

It was food first, then straight to Games's house, one step ahead of the rainstorm.

18
Bad and
Worse

Two days later we held what was to be our first and last
practice before Saturday's exhibition. We seemed to be
in a weird weather pattern, where it'd rain like crazy
during the day, every day, and not clear up till dinner
time. "A backwards frontwards system," I heard the
weatherman on TV say, or something like that. Whatever it was, he got me worrying about the possibility of
the big game being rained out. A delay meant playing
the following Saturday, or at least that was the plan. But
I had my doubts. Keyboard, I knew for sure, would be
on vacation. So would AD, whose family went away the
end of every summer. Other kids' families — Poisons,
too — ones I didn't know about, might be gone, also.
Mr. Sparkle would probably end up having to recruit
outsiders to play along with us, and the game, at least for
me, wouldn't be the same.

So I worried.

Wednesday, when there was a break in the storm, we
grabbed our equipment and sloshed out on the field for a

quick warm-up. The rain had made puddles of the dirt bases and pitcher's mound, so we moved downfield where the unmowed grass covered our shoe tops.

This time The Cinderella Kid showed up with his sister. He'd brought along a couple of his own bats, larger than the skinny broom handles we always used, and a glove the size of a walrus to fit over his enormous hand. AD started calling him "The Kid" out loud, and when he didn't snarl or complain, the rest of us picked up on it.

He was a pitcher, or had been before he'd beaned that kid. That much I knew from the newspaper article Olive had shown me and from what Games had said. Now that he'd decided to play, I wondered if he'd pitch for us, though I doubted it. I was right.

"It's your team," he told me, when I asked him. "I'll play wherever you want — except pitcher."

"How about . . . er . . . third b-base? Or outfield?" Wart suggested. He didn't want to give up his spot as catcher.

"Right field?"

"Sure," The Kid said.

We were still missing a third baseman, crucial for Saturday's game. The two kids I'd asked to play for us hadn't shown up, even though I'd told them about practice. They weren't what you'd call reliable and not very good players either, worse than Ping, but we needed somebody.

"Let's start without them," I said.

"Wait!" Olive shouted. "Here she comes now."

"She" was the Hemlock Street Poisons' second baseman, Socks, the puny girl with the green hair. I'd for-
gotten all about Olive's surprise player, who turned out
to be that — a surprise — and more.

"What gives, Olive?" I asked her.

"Socks's going to play for us."

"A Poison on McCarthy Road?" It seemed doubtful.
I wasn't even sure I wanted her.

"I'm not a Poison," Socks said in a chalky voice;
chalky, as in scraping a piece of chalk across a blackboard.
Olive and Socks were alike in more ways than one, and
both about the same age, eleven. "I don't even live on
Hemlock Street. I live two streets over. I was playing
for the Poisons because some of their team was away at
camp. Now they're back. They told me I was a . . .
bench winner."

"Warmer."

"Bench warmer. So I quit. Here I am."

That she was, baggy socks and all. She had a minuscule
glove on and was pounding her small fist in the pocket. I
kept remembering the two line drives she hit over my
head into the bush in right to help beat us in the last
game. Like Olive, for a kid her age, a girl, she could
definitely play.

"How're you at third?" I asked her.

"I can field," she answered. She looked as if I'd
insulted her. Her head, dunked in green glop, shone like
a plastic Christmas tree. All at once she bent over and
pretended to scoop up a grounder and fire it across an
imaginary diamond.

Olive and the others, even The Kid, laughed.

"You're on, Socks," I said. "Let's do fielding first, then hitting. Take your positions. I'll hit 'em out."

"Here," Wart said. He took a couple of baseballs out of his pants pockets and flipped them to me. Keyboard, Slam, and the others started running out to their positions. The Kid's loud voice stopped them.

"Wait a minute!" he said. "Those are hardballs. You play with tennis balls." The expression on his face looked as if he'd swallowed a live mouse, or had the worst practical joke in the world played on him.

"We do, usually," I said slowly. "But the exhibition is for next year's Pony League. Real baseball on a real field. Uniforms, umpires . . ."

Then it hit me. It was stupid of me not to have known. The only reason The Kid was out there at all was that we played with a tennis ball: less chance of anybody getting hurt. That was the problem, wasn't it? The Kid had taken a big step pinch hitting for me the other day, but we'd switched balls on him, and he was . . . heading home.

"Where in blazes is he going?" said AD.

"I-I don't get it," Wart said.

Slam started to say something, but Keyboard cut him off.

"What a coward."

"A lot you know!" Olive shouted at him. "You're the cowards! All of you!" She looked from one of us to the other, her face more fishlike than ever. Suddenly it turned a dark red and she started to cry. She picked up her glove and went home, trailing after her brother.

"Should be a great game Saturday," Keyboard said sarcastically.

When the clouds disappeared for the afternoon it was time to head for the Aquacenter. If my sore hand (which wasn't very sore) was good enough for mowing lawns, swinging a putter at the Minigolf, and hitting infield practice, it was certainly good enough for swimming. I'd used the injury and the rain as an excuse for staying clear of that part of town long enough. Don't get me wrong — I loved swimming; but going to the Aquacenter meant maybe running into Tom Jefferson. And if I ran into him I ran into a diving contest off the high board. Acrophobia, fear of heights. Wasn't that what AD had called it? Riding along, side by side on our bicycles, the memory of the swirling blue water made my skin itch with a thousand mosquito bites.

AD, more than anyone else, knew what I was going through.

"Maybe Jefferson won't be there," he said.

"He'll be there. Besides, I might as well get it over with."

"Then you're going through with it?"

I gave him a don't-be-stupid-of-course-I-am look.

"You don't have to."

"I do. He called me chicken pee-wee. It's either go off the high board or stop swimming for the rest of my life." I thought about that for a moment. "No," I said, pedaling to keep up, "there is no 'or'."

"There's always an 'or'," AD said.

But I pedaled even faster so I wouldn't have to hear him.

The town pool was jammed. Tons of kids had had the same idea as us, especially since the rain had kept the place closed for the last couple of days. The bike racks and parking lot were filled, the locker room was a cement sardine can. AD and I changed into our bathing suits and headed for the pool. Along the shallow end were places to spread out towels for sunbathing.

"Let's get some heat before we go in the water," I suggested, but AD wasn't paying attention.

"Jefferson's over by the diving area," he said. "Standing in line."

So he was. It was hard not to miss him: with his oversized body and loud mouth he was like a noisy, extra-large scoop of chocolate ice cream. There was a whole mess of kids, mostly guys, waiting to go off the high board with him, horsing around, pushing and shoving, friendly-like, the usual. Another long line snaked out behind the two low boards. There were mobs of half-naked people, kids and adults, everywhere.

"What're you going to do?" AD asked. He looked worried.

"Wait here for a while," I said. "Until the line's shorter. The fewer kids watching the better."

We spread our towels out on the hot cement and lay down. A kid I didn't know, a lot younger than I was, went leaping off the high board, feet first, flapping his arms like a lame duck, and hit the water with a splash. Almost at once another kid flew through the air, practically drowning the first kid, and got whistled at by the lifeguard, one of the ones who'd pried my hands off the board the last time I made the mistake of going up there. A few more kids dove off, bad divers, and then it was Jefferson's turn. The board bent a little under his weight, but when he took off it snapped upward, shooting him into the air. He did a front somersault, landing a little cockeyed and spraying water all over. His friends gave him a mock cheer.

"You're a better diver than he is," AD said matter-of-factly.

"Not up there."

"You're determined to go through with it?"

I nodded. There was no other way.

"Then here's what to do."

AD had some good suggestions. He told me to make sure Jefferson went first, so he wouldn't be right behind me mouthing off and making me even more uptight than I already was. He told me that from the time I started up the ladder to the time I hit the water at the end of my dive, I shouldn't look down. "Stare at something straight ahead," he said. "A treetop or the roof of a building. A cloud. Anything. Just don't look down." He also told me to do the easiest dive I knew and to think hard about doing it, picture it in my mind. "And go fast," he said. "Don't fool around up there."

He must've been giving my problem a lot of thought.

"Now's the time," I said, when he'd finished. "It's worse just waiting around."

"Do you want me to come, too?"

I shook my head at him and stood up, embarrassed.

Acrobat — acrophobia — whatever it is was sure a problem. "Wait here," I told him. "And try not to look."

I was glad Slam, Keyboard, and the others were late. The number of kids I knew who'd be watching was already too many, never mind the Basement Baseball Club who'd want to know what was wrong if I made a circus clown fool of myself, as I was sure to do. Olive and Socks, with silly grins on their faces, waved to me as I headed for the diving area, but I pretended not to notice. Instead I pulled the laces tighter on my bathing trunks. The last thing I needed was for the stupid thing to fall off when I hit the water.

Jefferson, in line again after his somersault, saw me coming.

"Look what I see," he said in an overly loud voice.

"Cut the crap, Jefferson," I said right back. "Let's go. You first."

"Wait a minute," he said. I want to make sure everybody knows what's happening. We need some judges, too."

I started to protest, but his booming voice swallowed my own.

"Diving contest, everybody! Me versus Carroll, here. One dive takes it all. Who wants to judge?"

He looked around at his group of friends, kids I knew, Ruff and a couple of other Poisons. Most of them were dripping with pool water, curious, grinning at Jefferson as much as me. "Who says *you* can dive, TJ?" one kid called out. The others laughed. Jefferson kept wetting his lips with his tongue. He was nervous, too. A small crowd had gathered, just what I didn't want. The lifeguard, a new one, kept moving the line along.

"So what if I can't dive?" Jefferson said, a wild smile smudging his face. "The thing is, against old Carroll here you don't have to. Just getting on the board's enough. Ain't that right, kid?"

Some of the others, kids who must've caught my last performance on the high board, were starting to figure things out. I could see it on their faces. What could I say?

"I'll be a judge," said Ruff.

"Me, too," said another kid.

"Who else?" Jefferson boomed. "One more judge to make three."

"Me. I'll do it."

The voice, deep and throaty, came from behind me. It was The Cinderella Kid, muscles like telephone wires. He had a towel around his shoulders and was leaning up against the lifeguard stand. A thin stream of water trickled off his nose.

"S . . . Sure," Jefferson said in a quieter voice, eyeing The Kid suspiciously. "Let's go to it."

"You first," I said.

"Anything you say," said Jefferson.

He put his foot on the bottom rung of the ladder. High above us a woman about my mother's age, wearing what looked like a two-man pup tent, took a couple of graceful hops and sprang out over the cool blue water in as perfect a swan dive as anybody'd ever see. Only her crooked toes caused a ripple when she landed. A swany, I told myself, remembering AD's advice. What could be easier than that?

Now it was Jefferson's turn. "See you at the asylum," he said, snickering. "I'll make sure all the lifeguards are on alert."

"Bacon-butt," I muttered.

"Chicken pee-wee."

Before I could answer he was up the steps, maybe ten of them, and over the top, his hands on the silver railings to steady himself before he made his final move. The line behind me and the surrounding group of kids pushed forward. I could feel them.

Then all at once Jefferson was away. SPRONGGG! He hit the board full speed and catapulted into the air. At the same time he grabbed onto his knees and spun forward in a try at another somersault, with the same results. Down he came, slamming into the water at a weird angle, partway on his side, with one leg sticking straight out, the other up around his chin, sort of like a wounded rhino. The enormous splash doused just about everybody, including the lifeguard, who looked ready to mangle him. "HUNGAAAH!"

Jefferson floated slowly to the surface, not eager to face what he knew was coming.

"Boooooo! Hisssss!"

"Let's see that on instant replay."

"On a scale of ten, minus seventy-two."

"Way to go, TJ!" Once again his friends gave him a mock cheer.

"Get moving," the lifeguard said to me. "Up or out of line."

On the far side of the pool, across the street, somebody'd put up a tall TV antenna on his roof. The top of the antenna was a rusty triangle. I zeroed in on it and headed up the metal steps of the diving board, one step after another. I tried to do what AD had told me, to go fast, but my feet just wouldn't listen. My hands held on tight to the railings. My skin itched and I could barely breathe, but up I went. Amazing, with all the people jammed into the place, but the only sound I could hear was the wind whipping my face. Jefferson or anybody else could've been yelling his head off and I wouldn't have heard him. I was all by myself.

Near the top step the antenna disappeared behind the diving board for an instant, then came back into view. I tried to think of the swan dive I was about to attempt, picture myself doing it, but all I could think of was what TV shows the people across the street were watching that would need such fancy equipment. Count to three and go, I told myself, right off the board and into the water. One . . . two . . . I took a deep breath and bit down hard on my lip . . . three!

I would've been okay if I hadn't tripped. One second I was on my way, running with my eyes closed, the next I was flat on my stomach, the stuffing knocked out of me, my head hanging out over the end of the board, face down. BONG! Like that — snap your fingers — the water began to swirl, faster and faster in a dizzying spin, an upside-down merry-go-round in flight and heading for the stars. A tarantula the size of a hand ran up and down my spine. A mad scientist had a vice around my head and sharp needles under my fingernails.

Look out below!

Somebody — Olive maybe — screamed out my name. At the same time the diving board began to shake. The lifeguards were coming to get me, like last time, pry my hands loose and drag me back along the board and down the steps to the safety of the ground. Never again would I be able to face up to Jefferson, or anybody else, if you want to know the truth, not even the Basement Baseball Club. And never again would I go anywhere near the Aquacenter. I'd be hearing "chicken pee-wee" for the rest of my life. In another second I was going to be sick. No, I couldn't let that happen to me, not for anything.

Somehow — a miracle — I managed to get to my knees, then to my feet, bent over like a tied roll of salami, my chin on the board, hanging on for all I was worth. The pool, a swirling blue bathtub, was about ten stories below me and fading fast. The sky, even with the sun out, seemed to grow dark, the wind buzzed in my ears. I shook all over, bouncing a little as the lifeguards came up behind me. Dive, Shooter! Dive! Was that my voice? It was.

I did — dive that is. That's all I remember.

When I came to there were a whole bunch of faces staring down at me, like something out of a horror movie. Their eyes were bugged out and their mouths were moving. They looked worried.

"He's all right," someone said. "Just swallowed a little water."

"W-Where am I?" I asked. What a jerk I was.

A couple of people, kids I think, laughed.

"You're in heaven," a voice said. It was AD. Now there was a lot of laughing.

An older kid, a lifeguard, helped me to my feet. When I saw where I was, on the cement walkway in the diving area, it all came back to me.

"You okay?" the lifeguard asked.

"Who won the contest?" I said, ignoring him.

"He's okay," AD assured him. He patted me on the back.

I was okay, except for the chlorine taste inside my mouth and a sore spot along the side of my face. Oh, yes, my chest burned. My head ached, like somebody'd been pounding on it with a fungo bat. I had cramps in both feet, my nose was bleeding, my eyeballs stung with sweat, and my front teeth felt like they were about to fall out. But that's all. Otherwise I was fine.

"Here, kid. Wipe your nose." The lifeguard handed me a towel. The circle of spectators, mostly kids, broke up and headed for the pool. One of them was The Cinderella Kid. Olive, who smiled at me and said something I couldn't hear, and Socks were with him. I saw Jefferson and his friends going off in the other direction. Good riddance.

"Come on," AD said. "Let's get out of here."

"What about the contest?" I said again. "Did I win or what?"

"Or what," said AD, giving me the eye. He looked funny without his glasses on, sort of like whipped cream without the cherry. "It was a tie. You both came in last."

"Last," I said incredulously. "What about the swany?"

"If that was a swan dive you did, then I'm starting center fielder for the White Sox."

Later, riding home on our bicycles, AD filled me in on the details.

"You looked pretty good going up the steps," he told me, "even though you were moving in slow motion. I could tell you were trying hard not to look down. At the top your face turned green as a . . . ripe cucumber. Your cheeks were puffing in and out. Kids were yelling for you to move it, but they all shut up at once when you fell on your face. The lifeguard jumped out of his chair and tried to push through the crowd of kids around the board. Olive screamed. Another lifeguard came and the two of them hustled up the steps, one after another. I was sure they were gonna have to drag you back like last time —"

"Gee, thanks," I said.

"Er . . . right," AD said, "but remember, I'd seen you black out in my bedroom. Anyway, before they got to you you'd pushed yourself up, sort of like a bug on a branch, your feet and face on the board, your butt skyward. Real funny. Then you took off. The lifeguard in front almost fell off the bouncing board. A couple of more kids screamed. It was very . . . er . . . entertaining."

"But what about the dive?"

"There was none, not like you're thinking. You never pulled out of your bug-on-the-branch position. Your face hit the water first and you went over on your back.

When you hit there was a loud WHAP! You got the same kind of cheer Jefferson got, a lot of laughs."

"Thanks again," I said.

"You know the rest." He shrugged.

"No, I don't. Who pulled me out of there?"

"Oh yeah. When you didn't come up right away, the two lifeguards dove in and hauled you out. They were thinking of giving you mouth-to-mouth when you came to. It all happened very fast. A couple of seconds is all. Oh, and one more thing. The lifeguards weren't the first to reach you in the water.

"Who was?"

AD smiled knowingly. "The Cinderella Kid," he said.

19
Two Wrongs Righted—
Maybe

When I got home I went straight to the refrigerator. Nothing like a quart of milk, four or five sweet rolls, a handful of chips, and some grapes, the seedless kind, to set things right. So what that I hadn't won the contest? I hadn't lost either, and I'd gone off the high board, hadn't I? So there. Jefferson could call me a lot of things, but he couldn't call me chicken, and even if he did, I knew better.

I was sitting at the kitchen table, reading the backs of my baseball cards and stuffing food into my mouth, when my mom pushed in through the swinging door. She was in the middle of doing what she always did after work on Wednesdays: playing in the world's longest mahjong game with her friends. It was either that or bridge. I could hear the rest of the ladies cackling on the other side of the wall. They were making so much noise they hadn't heard me scrounging around for my afternoon snack.

"Hi, Mom!"

"Oh, Shooter! You scared me. Where've you been,

swimming? What's that you're eating? Mrs. Ogilvie called and wants you to be sure to do her lawn before the weekend. Your dad won't be home until later tonight, so we'll wait to eat. Don't be a glutton in the meantime." She eyed my plate and made a face. "I see my suggestion is after the fact. What's that red mark on your face? Hmm?"

As she talked, rapid-fire, she was pulling things out of drawers, off the shelves, out of the freezer. Plates, napkins, forks, little round things that looked like frozen tarts of all different colors, diet soda, a can of beer, something red that fizzed.

"Who's pigging out?" I said, my mouth full of potato chips.

"Don't be fresh. Why is your face red? You've not answered."

"It's from diving off the high board," I said, but that was all. I'd already decided not to tell either of them, my mom or dad, about the acrophobia. They might decide to take me to a doctor, and I'd already seen enough doctors for one summer. Besides, what could a doctor do? It seemed like the kind of thing you'd just have to figure out on your own. I'd probably get around to telling them, but not before Saturday's game, and if they heard about the catastrophe from somebody else, I'd just make up an excuse. The Roaders already had enough problems.

"Try to be more careful," she said. "I'm not sure I like you going off the high board. Oh, I forgot," she was backing out through the swinging door, a huge tray of goodies in her hand, "there's someone waiting for you downstairs."

"Who?" My mom knew all my friends.

"Never saw him before. Very polite. Almost wouldn't wait for you to come home. I told him your presence wasn't required for him to wait in the basement. A big boy, very polite. You should get him to play —"

I snatched a couple of tarts and was down the stairs in an instant. The Cinderella Kid, his head scraping the ceiling, was standing awkwardly, shuffling from one foot to the other in the center of the room, surrounded by sports equipment, bowling pins, tipped-over folding chairs, jigsaw puzzle pieces, what was left of a dice-baseball game, Monopoly money, penants of most of the major league baseball teams. The Kid was holding a Ping-Pong paddle in his hand.

"Ice cream," I said, when he saw what I was eating. "Want some?"

He did, and swallowed an entire tart in one gulp.

"I need to know something," he said slowly, staring down at me. "What'd . . . Jefferson, I think that's his name, mean when he said that against you, just getting on the diving board was enough to win?"

I dropped what was left of my tart, went to pick it up, and instead stepped on it with my bare feet. "Twir-pitch!" The Cinderella Kid grinned nervously at me, waited for me to gouge strawberry ice cream out from between my toes.

"You don't have to tell me," he said.

"I know I don't." Then all of a sudden — don't ask

me why — I decided I would. After all, what'd I have to be embarrassed about? Nothing, that's what. As long as he didn't tell anybody else.

"Do you know what acro . . . phobia is?"

He shook his head and swung the Ping-Pong paddle at an imaginary ball.

"Fear of heights," I said.

"You?" He looked at me, surprised.

"Me. Don't tell anyone else."

"So that's it," he said knowingly, as if he'd already figured out that something was wrong. "Then how? Why?"

"I had to," I blurted out. "If you knew Jefferson, you would, too. He challenged me." I left out the part about the chicken pee-wee.

"You could've —"

I think he was going to say "gotten hurt," but he stopped himself.

"What'd you mean 'could've'?" I asked. "My whole body feels like it's ready for the garbage dump." It wasn't that bad, really.

The Kid handed me the paddle and headed for the stairs. His face looked weird, puzzled and sad at the same time, maybe a little angry. His eyebrows, like snarly bushes, had dropped down low over his eyes. One side of his face twitched. He cleaned out his ear with his finger.

"Did you know about the . . . fear? Ahead of time, I mean?" he asked.

"Oh, sure." I tried to sound as "no sweat" as I could.

He shook his head, more puzzled than ever.

"Don't tell anyone, okay?" I said again.

"I won't," he said. "Not even my sister."

I decided right then and there to take a big chance with him. "What about Saturday?" I asked him.

He answered me in a voice as quiet as a frog with laryngitis. "You mean the game? I . . . er . . . well . . . er . . . I . . . count me in. Right field."

"You're sure? It's hardball."

"I'm sure."

WHOOP-DE! Now we were talking.

I slept for about twenty hours. When I woke up it was raining again, washing out another practice, but for once that was okay. I had something important I wanted to do, and headed over to Games's house to do it. It'd been three days since the Basement Baseball Club, AD mostly, had come up with the brilliant plan to get Games out of his house, in a way that his mother probably wouldn't mind at all. It'd been a lot longer, almost two weeks, since he'd been allowed to do anything with his friends. His mother meant business.

Here's what had happened after our golfing match. The four of us — AD, Keyboard, Slam, and myself — went straight from the Minigolf to Games's back door. His mother had to let us in because there was thunder and lightning outside. She wasn't real pleased, but when we — I — told her our plan she perked up.

"Say that again," she said. Games, looking as comical as ever, with his light-socket haircut, was there with her.

"The guy at the Minigolf is looking to give a kid a job," I explained, slower than the first time. "He asked

if any of us wanted it, but we don't. We told him about
Games and he said to tell him — you, Games — to come
see him. Good pay, good hours."

"Flexible," said AD.

"What kind of job?" Mrs. Murphy asked. I could
see by the look on her face — her pretty face — that she
was skeptical.

"He said maintenance: lawn mowing, painting, being
a handy man."

Mrs. Murphy still looked skeptical. Games wasn't
talking, probably for the first time in his life. Two weeks
of being grounded was taking its toll.

"Minigolf?" Mrs. Murphy asked. "You mean that
place up the highway?"

We all nodded.

"I don't know," she said. "What do you think, Paul?"

"Sounds good to me," Games said, trying not to sound
desperate. I guess anything was better than what he'd
been doing, stuck inside the house with his mother day
after day. Still, he was the one who caused the trouble.

His mother didn't say anything. She was thinking
hard. No one else said anything either. The faucet drip-
ped in the sink. A cat meowed. It was hard not to laugh,
but I got control of myself by biting my lip. I wished
I had a piece of gum.

"Well," Mrs. Murphy said, finally, "I guess there's no
harm in finding out for ourselves. When would the job
start?"

"Soon," I said. "Today. The man said to hurry."

"Paul?" His mother looked at him.

"Sure," he said.

Turned out Games got the job. Now it was three days later and I was curious to find out how he was doing and if there was any chance, no matter how puny, of him pitching for us on Saturday. I had to wait for my answer because he wasn't home. "He's at work," his mom told me. She was smiling, I guess you'd say cautiously, as if she knew a secret but wasn't telling.

"Work? But it's raining."

"He goes rain or shine," she said. "I take him there and pick him up myself. I'll tell him you stopped by, Shooter."

"Thanks."

I decided, rain or no rain, that I'd better find things out for myself, and since no one else was around to go with me, that's just what I did. A half-hour later, a waterlogged prune, I pulled up on my bike outside the Minigolf. A sign on the fence said in big letters CLOSED. A few people inside the fast-food restaurant, a lot drier than I was, watched me climb the steps toward the course entrance. I looked past the sign. Everything was in its place — Vomit Belch, Fried Eggs, Zip Your Lip — only no one was around. No one. The shack where the man with the diamond earring gave out the balls and putters was locked up tight. Why not? Only an idiot would play golf on a day like this, or be doing what I was doing.

Time to leave.

"Psssst, Shooter! Over here!"

"Games!"

He was waving to me from just inside the door of the shack. I tried the latch on the gate. It was open. "What're you doing here? The place is closed."

"Working." He pushed the door open for me as I scrambled past him. Once inside I shook the water off my raincoat like a soggy dog.

"Whaddaya mean working?" I said. "It's raining out." And then I saw for myself. He *was* working. There were a bunch of boards of all sizes in a big pile in the middle of the floor. Games was painting them white. "They're for the driving range my boss is building behind this place," Games told me. "He says I can run this place — the Minigolf — all by myself after school an' on weekends when I'm not busy. He'll run the driving range an' the fast food. He owns that place, too."

"You mean that guy with the diamond in his ear?"

"Yep." He was smiling crookedly. He'd smeared white paint all over his face and down the front of his shirt. His bare legs were polka dotted. Inside the shack, which was boarded up tight and had an echo, his voice sounded like a cat fight. Putters and golfballs were everywhere.

"I never knew you liked work so much, Games."

"I don't. Not really. But I like money, an' this guy's paying me a whole lot more than my mom was. Besides, when the rain stops, mostly I'll be working outdoors. I'm not hanging around home getting on my mom's nerves an' her getting on mine. An' I get to eat for free, burgers, shakes, you name it."

Now that *was* something! And to think I'd turned the job down.

"You probably get to play for free, too," I said enviously.

"Yep." Games grinned some more. "An' on special occasions I may just be able to get the club in with me."

Three days of work had sure changed him . . . or had they? In some ways I was glad. In others. . . . One look at the sloppy mess he'd made of himself told me that deep down he was still Games, the wild man we all knew and liked.

"What about Saturday's game?" I asked him, coming to the point.

His grin disappeared.

"Don't know yet," he answered. "It's still too early to tell."

"Too early! The game's the day after tomorrow and you're supposed to be our starting pitcher."

"Look," he said. "I know my mom. She's happy 'cause I like this job an' the guy who hired me likes me — he told her so himself. But I don't know. She said I couldn't play ball for the rest of the summer. If it was a few more weeks from now maybe, but —"

"Have you asked her?"

"No, but I will at dinner tonight, if she's in a good mood. Otherwise tomorrow. I'll let you know."

He did. That same night. And the answer was still the same: maybe.

Get ready, Keyboard!

20
The Game
Was On

Saturday at last! My eyes popped open like a couple of squeezed zits and got zapped by sunlight. One of my main worries was over: it wasn't raining, anything but. In fact, the sun was so bright coming in through the bedroom window that I'd been dreaming I'd fallen asleep sunbathing on my back at the Aquacenter.

Mr. Sparkle had called to ask me to stop by the Candy Shack, along with the rest of the Roaders, before we showed up at the park where the village picnic was being held, alongside Indianwood Field, the best baseball diamond in town. He wanted to give us our shirts and hats for the game. The backs of the shirts were supposed to have SPARKLE's written on them.

Keyboard, who had changed his Saturday piano lesson from afternoon to morning, couldn't come early. Neither could Games, who still — if you can believe this — didn't know if his mother was going to let him play or not. "If I'm there, I'm there," he told me on the phone. The Cinderella Kid couldn't make it either, not early. He'd told Olive to tell us he'd meet us at the field. Maybe

he was still embarrassed about quitting practice the day
he'd found out about the hardballs. He shouldn't have
been.

When I'd told the Roaders The Kid had changed his
mind about playing, they practically went crazy. There
was loud cheering and I got pounded on the back as if
I'd had something to do with it. Maybe in a way I had.
Even Keyboard, who I thought might be jealous (after
all, he was our best player) seemed relieved that The
Kid'd be playing. He wanted to beat the Poisons as
much as I did. "I'd like to see that sucker kick Bull's
behind!" he'd shouted at the news.

Mr. Sparkle was waiting for us when we got there, his
bald head shining like the aluminum Sno-Kone machine.
"Good morning, Roaders!" he sang out. Olive and
Socks, who didn't know Mr. Sparkle at all and weren't
used to his enthusiasm, started to giggle. So did Ping,
Keyboard's younger brother and our extra player in case
we were a man short. I knew Ping didn't really want to
play, but our only other choice was to get a kid from
another neighborhood or somebody we didn't know
from the picnic. And if we beat the Poisons using
strangers they'd more than likely claim that the game
didn't count. No, Ping was it. I wasn't taking any
chances.

Mr. Sparkle pulled a couple of cardboard boxes out
from underneath the counter.

"Try these on for size," he said, handing them over.

We did. They were green T-shirts and matching hats.
There was a mad scramble not to be left out, though
there were more than enough uniforms to go around.

After I'd found ones that fit me and everybody else seemed ready, I put the four or five uniforms that were left back inside one of the boxes and tucked it, along with my glove, under my arm. The Kid, Keyboard, and Games, if he made it, would thank me.

With our uniforms on, T-shirts over regular shirts, we looked like what we were — a team. My stomach rumbled. Was it full or empty? My fingers itched. Every sweat pore in my body was wide open and working, even in the air-conditioned store. All good signs, or so I'd learned in gym class, something about adrenal glands. Or was it adenoids? Olive's green hat tilted lopsidedly on her head, as usual. Along with her strawberry hair and nose she looked like Christmas, but you know what? For some reason — don't ask me — the sight of her in her baseball uniform got my adrenaline going even more. My confidence soared. We were gonna win!

"I bet some of your parents are busy this morning," said Mr. Sparkle. Right he was. My mom and dad, Slam's mom, and AD's parents were all hot-footing it around, scrounging up supplies for the afternoon's picnic. Probably so were hundreds of other parents. Edgewater Township was known for its . . . what's the saying? Community spirit.

The doorbell jingled, a few little kids came in with their parents, bought some candy and sodas, and left.

"There are only seven of you," Mr. Sparkle said, heading back down toward our end of the store. I guess he hadn't noticed that I'd taken the extra shirts and hats. "Do you need more players?"

"Two or, er . . . three others are coming later," I told him.

"Good," he said. "With the help of some of your parents, I've managed to get almost all the village councilors to attend the game, and some of the local merchants, too. I don't think we'll have any trouble at all next year with the sponsors. And now that word has gotten out, several people — your dad included, Slam — have expressed an interest in coaching. Sure you and the Poisons don't want some coaches for the exhibition? Last chance."

"We already have a coach, Mr. Sparkle," AD said, slapping me on the back. "Old Shooter here. If he coaches, then no matter how bad he is he'll always get to play."

The rest of the Roaders laughed. So did Mr. Sparkle. "What about the Poisons?"

"They've got a coach, too," I said.

"A team of coaches," put in Socks. She would know.

"Then that settles it," Mr. Sparkle said. "Except for the umpire — me — you're on your own." From behind the counter he pulled out a blue umpire's chest-protector and mask and a few more boxes, uniforms for the Poisons. "Good luck, and I'll see you later."

The picnic, almost everybody said afterward, was a superfine success. And why shouldn't it have been? First off, there was just about anything anyone could want to eat and drink, though I myself concentrated on the grilled hamburgers, sloppy joe tacos, cheese and mushroom pizza, soft ice cream, and a cold Dr. Pepper or two, and tried not to get too filled up. I kept a lookout for what the others were eating (I was the coach, wasn't I?), especially Wart, who at a picnic could be expected to behave like a frenzied whale who'd just ended a starvation diet. One time, when we were younger, Wart had won a school-wide miniature-pie-eating contest by putting down — swallowing whole was more like it — about fifty of those rosin-bag-size pies, all different flavors, in less time than it would take a normal person to polish off a hamburger and a Coke. I'd seen Wart waste all his allowance and a chunk of the weekly money he made washing cars in one short sitting at the fast food. He could down a quart of soda faster than the time it took Bull Reilly's fast ball to reach home plate. No exaggeration. I'd seen him do it with my own eyes.

"You don't need to s-spy on m-me," he told me with a hurt look on his face. He was holding a hot dog, mustard and ketchup, buried under a mound of smelly sauerkraut, in each hand. "This is my last one . . . er, two."

Turned out they were. He wanted to be ready to play, too. We all did.

I saw Bull wandering around the picnic grounds with Jefferson and Freedburg and their fathers, toting baseball gloves and bats and helmets like we were. Freedburg saw me over by the soft drink table and half-waved, then rudely turned his back. As I'd heard the White Sox announcer say, "No fraternizing with the enemy." At least not on game day.

It was hot as blazes out, and many of the picnickers were stretched out under trees, where it was shady but

not much cooler, or on the grass or lawn chairs they'd
brought from home. Some sat at picnic tables. Others,
like myself, just wandered slowly around. A bunch of
people, kids mostly, were wearing bathing suits, probably on their way to the Aquacenter when the picnic
was over. All told, there must've been a thousand of us
("More like two thousand," said my dad afterward).
The junior high school band, looking barbecued and
bewildered as ever, kept up a steady racket of marching
music, the Cub Scouts and Brownies ran around handing
out "I ♥ E.T." buttons (our home town, not the extra-
terrestrial), and overweight ladies, who must've been
members of the ladies' auxiliary, barked out the sched-
ule of events through king-size megaphones.

There were fun rides for the little kids, such as a
merry-go-round and miniature Ferris wheel about as
high as a jungle gym, a three-sided rubber room called
"The Bouncer," for bouncing on without your shoes,
and some weary-looking ponies, their tails swatting flies.
You could smell them clear across the park. In the middle
of lunch the village fire department showed off by res-
cuing a Siamese cat that'd gotten stuck at the top of a
tree. You can probably guess how it got there in the first
place. The Rec, which had supplied the picnic tables
and gotten the baseball field in shape — no easy chore
after all the rain — organized some relay races, but I
didn't enter any (AD and Olive did) because I didn't
want to get worn out before the game. Somebody won a
set of encyclopedias in the afternoon's raffle, someone
else won a free haircut, and an old lady, the luckiest
person alive, won two box seats to see the White Sox at

Comiskey Park. Maybe, if I played my cards right, she'd take me. Probably not.

The whole world exploded just before game time. No, there weren't any fireworks. It was daytime, remember? What I'm saying is that the notorious troublemaker, Bad News Paul "Games" Murphy, showed up. And get this: he was *with* his mother. ("It was the only way she'd let me play," Games told me later. "She wants it so she can keep an eye on me when I'm not working. Besides, she wanted to see me play. So did my boss.") That's right, the guy with the diamond in his ear showed up, too, and sat with Mrs. Murphy in the bleachers. I could guess what he was up to.

When I saw Games, ten steps out in front of his mother, I practically did a back flip, without even using The Bouncer.

"I don't believe it!" I shouted.

"Yes," Games said, pretending to be cool, as if he'd known he'd be coming all along, "I am here." Then he sneezed, once, twice, about ten times. His face broke into a crooked smile, and all at once he howled crazily, sounding his old self, like a cat fight.

I was so happy I wanted to slug him.

"Let's get the others and take infield practice before the Poisons do," I suggested.

"Whatever happened to the —"

"There he is now," I said. It was The Cinderella Kid. And Keyboard, the two of them walking across the parking lot. Things sure were looking up.

The game was on.

21
The One That Counted Most

The flip of a coin, which the Roaders won, decided who would be home team and bat last. At a signal from Mr. Sparkle, the umpire behind the plate, we ran out on the field.

"Let's get 'em! WHOOP-DE! Fungofandanglefat!"
We could've all been playing for the White Sox.

Right off, Slam, our first baseman, began tossing easy warm-up grounders to the infielders: besides myself, Olive at second and Socks, who it turned out had a decent arm, at third. The regulation size infield was larger than the sandlot ones we were used to playing on behind our houses. But that didn't matter. My practice throws across the diamond were on a line and accurate, landing in Slam's glove with a reassuring slap. My stomach kept up its rumble — maybe I hadn't gotten enough to eat — and I was out of breath with the jitters, but I knew that'd end as soon as the game got under way. To help, I stuffed a wad of gum in my mouth and worked on it. Everyone on the field, including the Poisons over by their dugout, was chattering away — "Let's go! Take it to 'em! They're nothin'!" — a sign that the others were feeling the same.

"Batter up!" Mr. Sparkle hollered.

Freedburg, first up for the Poisons, did exactly what I knew he would. Choking up on the bat, he bunted Games's first pitch, a hard fast ball, down the third base line. He wasn't wasting any time testing Socks in her new position, just like his teammates had done to me when they'd found out I'd hurt my hand and couldn't throw. I'd warned Socks ahead of time, so she was playing it safe, inside the bag. She came charging in, fielded the bunt on the bounce, planted her feet, and threw to first, all in one motion. Dead perfect. Out number one. "Take that, suckers," I said under my breath.

Two quick outs later we were up.

Indianwood Field was about as major league as Edgewater Township got. Because of the rain and the electrical storms, the Recreation Department had had to wait until the morning of the game, that very morning, to get the field in shape. I knew. Along with AD and Slam, I had come by the field almost every day, in the rain, to take a look. The Rec had done a real good job. The infield and pitcher's mound — a real mound, not like our dirt spot at home — had been swept smooth, and the outfield grass mowed. The base lines, from home plate to the corners in right and left field, as well as the batter's boxes, had been chalked white. The five-foot-high wooden outfield fence had been repaired in a couple of spots. The Rec had even cleaned out the dugouts, two stone lean-tos with slate roofs. One of my favorite things about playing at Indianwood was the smell inside the dugouts, a mixture of warm dirt, sweat, and oily leather. I could smell dugout in my sleep.

Bull looked scary. On the raised mound he was even more gigantic than usual, forget that he stood farther away, Pony League distance. His warm-up pitches were pounding Jefferson's mitt. You could hear WHAP! WHAP! all over the field, which made getting up to hit against him all the harder. Very impressive, at least the people watching from the stands thought so. I could hear them murmuring every time Bull chucked one. I tried to figure out how many spectators there were, probably all left over from the picnic, but there were too many to count. No question, it was the largest crowd I'd ever played before, and I think it gave me an extra shot of adrenaline. I did spot my dad sitting with Slam's dad, Mr. Sanders, and AD's mom. She waved when she saw me looking. I popped her a bubble.

"Batter up!"

Suddenly, there I was, the McCarthy Roaders' lead-off hitter, in the batter's box, facing the meanest pitcher who ever lived. I tapped the plate three times with my bat for good luck and got into my crouch. Behind me Jefferson flashed the sign; Mr. Sparkle got set to call the pitch. The fielders hollered at Bull, my own teammates gave it to me — "Hit it, Shooter! Meet that ball! No pitcher! No pitcher!" Bull rocked once on the mound, kicked his leg high in the air, and fired, overhand. The ball, a white blur out of Bull's red-shirt background, dropped out of the sky. No, not dropped — sizzled.

Szzzzzzzippp!

"Strike one!" Mr. Sparkle let loose with a loud one

and Jefferson echoed, "Strike one!" He was talking away back there, nonstop nonsense about all sorts of things, mostly about how I couldn't hit a dead fly with a sledge hammer, junk like that, but I didn't have time to listen. Bull's next pitch, another sizzler, was on its way. The fast ball went by me and into the catcher's mitt before I'd swung and missed.

"Strike two!"

"Come on, Shooter! Choke up on the bat!" It was my dad. Funny how you can hear your own parents' voices when all the hundreds of others sound the same.

I took his advice, choked up even more than I had, and concentrated on meeting the ball. Bull, all six feet of him, scowled in at Jefferson for the sign, no doubt another fast ball, let loose with a wad of brown spit (I wonder what he had for lunch), rocked, and fired. Szzzzzzzzippp! CRACK! The speed of the pitch tore the bat from my hands, but I hit it on a line to first. Big Foot caught it without moving. One out.

"You'll get it next time, Shooter!" my dad called out.

I felt excited, the sweat pouring down my face and arms, my heart beating out a tune. I hadn't struck out. Maybe we could lick this monster after all.

The Cinderella Kid, batting sixth, came up for the first time with two out in the second, the game still scoreless. I yelled, hollered, whistled, shrieked, and catcalled every bit of encouragement I could from my seat inside the dugout. My teammates did the same. "GOOOOOOOO, KIIIIIIIID!" I had to admit, The Kid looked impressive. He was definitely a match for Bull, though he didn't have Bull's wicked scowl or habits, the spitting and snorting, to name two. He didn't sweat like a broken water main either, but he did have Bull's hands. When The Kid gripped the bat, even one the size of a tree trunk supplied by the Rec, it looked broom-handle puny.

The Kid. Ever since warm-ups I'd been keeping a close eye on him. He wasn't the sort to do a lot of hollering, not even to psych himself up. In fact, he hardly said anything, just a couple of whispers to Olive before her first at bat (she'd struck out). He did hustle out to his position in right field, his official green hat tilted sideways, the way his sister wore hers, only over the opposite ear, and he made a nice running catch on a long fly ball to end the Poisons' half of the first inning. He was graceful, effortless, a true athlete. From the look on his face — red and twitchy, as if somebody had his hands around his throat — I tried to figure out what he was feeling. Worried was too easy a word for it. Scared? Maybe. Uncomfortable, sad, troubled, nervous — whatever it was, it was weirding him out.

"Come on, Kid!"

His first time up The Kid headed for the plate as if he'd just been told to swallow a whole bottle of milk of magnesia. Any fool could see that for him, batting was going to be as hard as, say, pitching. He stood tall enough, same as before, his knees and arms locked in place, bat high and straight, only he looked too locked, too straight. So much of hitting was being relaxed. He wasn't. Anything but.

"Strike the bum out!" Jefferson shouted. His team-mates picked up the chant. "Bum, bum, bum, bum!" One more out and the inning was over.

"Hit it, John!" Olive squeaked. Her pink tongue was out.

"Strike one! Strike two! Strike three!"

The Kid hadn't moved, not even to blink. In fact, he wasn't moving now. Mr. Sparkle had to tell him twice he was out and give him a little push before he came slowly back to the dugout, dropped his bat in the dirt, picked up his glove, and trotted slowly with his head down, out to his position in right. "Harumph!" Keyboard said dis-gustedly, while AD gave me one of his raised-eyebrow looks, as if to say, "What now?"

It took the Poisons four innings to break the ice. Games, who'd struck out six of the Poisons' first nine batters — "Go get 'em, Games!" — got a little cute with Jefferson, throwing him a curve ball on a 3–2 count, and walked him. A wild pitch in the dirt moved Jefferson to second. A Bull fly ball to right (The Kid making another good catch) got him over to third.

Big Foot, up next, hit a slow roller back to the mound. Games charged in, as Jefferson lumbered like an over-loaded van toward the plate. Wart, knocking off his mask, lurched forward. Jefferson, Wart, and the ball all arrived at the exact same time. There was an awful THUD!, a monster collision that sent players sprawling. The ball bounced free. Jefferson was safe with the first run of the game, Poisons, 1–0.

"Time!"

Wart hauled himself up out of the dirt and dust and

base line chalk, looking his usual, a mess. I could tell he was disgusted with himself, and a little embarrassed. He'd had the ball in his mitt, but had dropped it. The Poisons, meanwhile, pounded their own catcher on the back. "Jeff-er-son! Jeff-er-son!" Some kids who must've been friends of his began chanting his name from the stands. He tipped his hat at them and flashed a smile.

"Batter up."

Oh, yeah. The inning wasn't over yet, not until the Poisons got two more hits and I made an error on a pop fly that got lost in the glare of the sun (it almost landed on my head), which put us into even deeper trouble, down 3–0 before a grounder to Slam ended it.

Bull, as you might expect, was mowing the Roaders down, one after another. By the seventh inning he'd struck out eleven batters, including me once. The Kid, except for his perfect fielding, was a lost cause, a bummer. He'd been up twice and had struck out both times, never once swinging. He seemed to go numb at the plate, his face white as rosin, his bat locked into position as, one after another, Bull's fast balls sizzled by. "Swing, John. You can do it!" someone yelled from the stands. At first I didn't recognize the voice; then I did. It was The Kid's mother. "Swing, Kid!" a couple of our players joined in, including me, but it was no use. Three strikes and he was out.

In our half of the seventh we finally got something going. Up till then Bull had been working on a perfect game, eighteen outs in a row, no hits for us, no walks. No base runners. "Choke up, Shooter!" my dad reminded me again as I stepped up, his voice rising above the others.

I already was choking up, but I moved my hands up an inch or two more, and with the count 0–2 against me, rapped a single up the middle. "Way to go!" AD followed with a hard grounder to Big Foot at first, a sure double play, but she muffed it for an error. Two on, no outs, the tying run, Olive, at the plate.

Bull bore down. After calling time, he stalked off the mound, used the rosin bag to dry his sweaty hands and arms, reset his hat low over his eyes, then, once again, toed the rubber. Six pitches and two strike-outs later, base runners AD and I still hadn't moved. "Zapashuca-marmalade!" Keyboard growled in disgust, after his third straight swing and miss. He was trying too hard.

Slam, it turned out, wasn't. Batting lefty as always, he worked the count to 2–1 in his favor, took aim, and hit a rising fast ball on a line to deep right center. There being two outs, I tore down the base line, rounded third, and headed for home, at the same time taking a quick look over my shoulder to pick up the flight of the ball. No question at all, it was out of here, a home run to tie the game.

No, it wasn't. CLUNK! The sound of the ball hitting the top of the fence and bounding into play came shooting back at me. Ruff, playing center, ran the ball down and pegged it to the infield. Slam slid into third with a two-run triple. Poisons, 3–2. The people in the stands seemed to come alive now that it was a close game again, at least those rooting for the Roaders. Our bench was up and screaming. "WHOOP-DE! Slam, the man!" Our lead run was now at the plate — The Cinderella Kid.

"Strike one!"

Just like that — blink! — a fast ball zipped through the air and landed in Jefferson's mitt with a loud WHAP! What did The Kid do? Exactly the same thing he did his last two times up: stood at the plate, unmoving as a frozen piece of salami. "You gotta swing to hit it, Kid!" I shouted. What the twirpitch was wrong with him? As if I didn't know.

"Swing! You can do it! Swing! Swing!"

The crowd picked up the chant.

"Strike two!"

I gave a quick look to AD, who was standing on the steps at the opposite end of the dugout. He shook his head at me despairingly. I knew what he — what we all — were thinking. This might be our one and only chance to tie the game up, even take the lead against the hated Poisons.

"Time!" Was that my voice? It was, the croak of a sick frog. As the Roaders' coach, I had to do something, even if it was only to stall.

"What is it, Shooter?" Mr. Sparkle asked from behind his mask, as I headed toward the plate.

"I . . . er (cough) . . . want a conference with The Kid."

"Make it short."

The Kid had backed out of the batter's box. I pulled him aside, up the third base line, out of ear shot. A few yards away stood Bull, a mound of muscle and sweat, glaring down at me. Who was I, some pip-squeak nothing of a kid, to be holding up the game?

"You gotta swing, Kid," I said encouragingly, under my breath.

The Kid just shook his head. He wouldn't look at me. His face was as white and shiny as a brand new baseball, the look on it even scarier than Bull's. After watching The Kid bat a couple of times, the Poisons had begun to call him Zombie and Mr. Statue and Granite Face, but he really wasn't any of those, not at all. You could see it right there, in his eyes, the way his face twitched and his lips wobbled. He was scared silly, no matter what he or Olive had told me about his not wanting to hurt some-body else. He was afraid of being hurt, too. That's why down in my basement, he'd asked me about the acro-phobia. That's why....

I grabbed his elbow. At that moment he seemed a whole lot younger than thirteen.

"Try," I said.

"Get someone else," he whispered.

"There is no one else. And even if I could, I wouldn't." Was that true? Probably not. More than anything I wanted to win the game. Didn't I? But when the words came out they sounded true. I wanted him to be the one to do it, win or lose.

The Kid's eyeballs stopped jumping around and he stared angrily at me. I was the only one outside his family, not counting some doctor, who knew his secret.

"Then you're a jerk," he said. "You. Everybody."

"One swing," I said. "Win or lose." He shook his head. "Then don't — coward!"

I couldn't help myself. The words, like before, just came out. The Kid's nose, already a strawberry, grew redder. He stumbled backward, the bat slipping off his shoulder and falling to the ground. He went to pick it up, but accidentally kicked it over to Jefferson. "Here, Zombie," Jefferson said, handing it to him. The Kid never said a word.

"Play ball!" Mr. Sparkle shouted.

I was almost too scared to watch. Almost. Good thing, because if I'd closed my eyes I'd have missed all the excitement.

Bull's first pitch after the time-out, the hardest pitch he'd thrown all day — Szzzzzzzzippp! — did what no talking could ever have done. The pitch hit The Cinderella Kid square in the chest with a crunch as loud as an auto wreck. The Kid, his bat and helmet flying, nose-dived on top of the plate. He kicked and moaned like an animal who'd got its leg caught in a trap. He rolled around in the dirt, too hurt even to grab the sore spot. He gurgled and spit. Then, horribly, he lay still. I held my breath.

A whole lot of things happened at once. Mr. Sparkle fired his mask halfway across the infield, screamed, "Doctor!" and shoving Jefferson aside, fell on top of The Kid as he tried to help him. Bull came running in from the mound, Olive shot out of the dugout, with yours truly and the rest of the Roaders a step or two behind. The people watching from the stands may as well have been in church, they were that quiet, on their feet, their faces showing concern. My dad, Slam's dad, The Kid's mom and dad were on the move behind the screen, heading for the plate. "Somebody call an ambulance!" I heard someone shout, but it wasn't necessary.

No sooner had things looked their worst, when they looked their best. A second before the mob of people reached Mr. Sparkle and the wounded — dead? — batter, The Cinderella Kid, his head and body a brown blob of dirt, leaped to his feet, more alive than ever and angry as a hungry hornet. "Nice pitch, idiot!" he screamed at Bull, and took a step toward him. I swear, if the two of them had started fighting, it would've been like one of those movies where two prehistoric dinosaurs duel to the death. Bull's mouth dropped open, more, I'm sure, from being startled at The Kid's quick recovery, than from being afraid of him.

"Are you all right, son?" Mr. Sparkle asked.

"Sure," The Kid answered, still staring at Bull, who was staring right back.

"Positive, John?" It was The Kid's father.

"Aw, leave me alone, all of you," said The Kid. A fierce smile had crept across his face. His lips were curled, baring his teeth. His eyebrows sunk, hiding his eyes. His fists kept clenching and unclenching. He looked mean enough to bite somebody's head off. Suddenly, he scooped his filthy batting helmet out of the dirt, shoved it down over his mop of hair, and headed for first base. He was a hit batter, wasn't he?

The crowd of us, all but Bull, who went back to the mound, watched him go. "Well, I'll be —" Mr. Sparkle started to say, as surprised as the rest of us. Olive was dumbfounded, her pink tongue in and out like a snake. "Whaddaya think?" Mr. Sparkle asked The Kid's father. "Maybe we should have a doctor take a look."

"He looks okay to me," The Kid's father, Mr. Johnson, said. "Must've just stunned him."

"Then let's play ball!"

"Who's up?" I asked, not that it mattered. For before Bull even threw a pitch, he caught Slam leading too far off third base and picked him off, ending the inning. So much for the tying run. So much for the lead. I saw The Kid rub his chest only once, on his way out to right field to start the eighth inning. He had fire in his eyes.

22
The End of the
Beginning

The tension kept building on every pitch. In the eighth, Games, who I knew must've been tiring, hung tough. He walked the first two batters he faced, a sure sign of fatigue; but he got the pip-squeak kid to hit into a force play, and got both a kid I didn't know (who'd taken Socks's place in their line-up) and Freedburg to pop up. No harm done.

None by us either, I'm sorry to say.

Wouldn't you know it? In the ninth, Bull hit a monstrous homer over the outfield fence, a ball hit so hard that AD barely had time to flinch before the ball soared over his head, over the fence, gone. The ball landed out by the duck pond, a long, long way away. Some little kids chased it and had a fight trying to decide who'd throw it back in. Mr. Sparkle pulled another shiny white baseball out of his oversized umpire's pocket and threw it back in play. The Poisons mobbed Bull, screaming and pounding him on the back as he crossed home plate. The spectators gave him a hand. No doubt about it, he was a super player, tough as a tank. As a salute, he spit a brown blob of saliva in the dirt on his way back to the dugout and grinned, showing every one of his teeth. Games looked rattled.

"One more out," I reminded him. "You can do it."

He could. The top of the inning ended with the Poisons ahead, 4–2.

The bottom of the ninth was our last chance, a whole summer of baseball come down to this. Bull, who'd been throwing extra hard the whole game in the blazing heat, started tiring, too, just like Games. That was easy to understand. He was super, but he wasn't Superman. His fast ball still sizzled and crackled, but he began to get wild. He walked me, leading off, on four pitches, not one of them near the plate. I practically danced down the base line in disbelief. Bull rarely walked anyone.

"Don't get picked off!" Keyboard warned, remembering Slam.

There was no chance of that, not now. I stayed close to the bag, watching carefully as AD, the tying run, walked as well. He looked as disbelieving as I had, flipping the bat above his head toward the home dugout on his way by. From the stands, his mother let loose with a shrill cry that sounded like a starving sea gull who'd just spotted its dinner. She let out another blast when Olive, nose to her knees, walked on a 3–2 count, a close pitch that could've gone either way. In other words, she could've been called out.

Bull came off the mound in a hurry and grabbed the rosin bag with his huge hand, knuckles the size of eggs. His red baseball shirt was soaked through. A rip showed under his muscular arm. He glared disgustedly at Mr.

Sparkle, but, true to form, said nothing, at least not to the umpire. He muttered something under his breath, probably a couple of swears.

"You can do it, Bull!" some parent shouted from the stands. "No batter! No batter! Bull! Bull! Bull! Bull!"

Keyboard stepped in, but before Bull pitched the ball he gave me, the runner at third, a disdainful look that said, "Go ahead, runt, make a move for home." Then he spit in my direction, scowled in at Jefferson for the sign, wheeled, and fired. Keyboard swung — THONK! — and hit a bullet, foul, down the line, a ball that had me diving for cover. "Straighten it out, Keyboard!"

He tried, you gotta give him that, hitting the next pitch almost as hard but straight to Freedburg, who, after gloving it, missed doubling a sliding AD at second by a bird turd.

"Safe!" the bases umpire, a friend of Mr. Sparkle's, hollered, giving the palms-down sign with his hands. Whew!

"Stay alive, AD!"

Now there was one out, with Slam at the plate. My first thought, a daydream if ever there was one, when I saw him hefting his bat, was another shot off the wall, a three-run triple this time, a game winner. I could tell he was still a little down on himself for having been picked off third two innings ago. "You can do it, Slam!" I yelled encouragingly, but, like Keyboard, although he tried hard, he couldn't. On a 3-2 count (the tension was so great I could barely watch), he hit a soft looper off the end of the bat that Big Foot caught in foul territory in front of our dugout. Now there were two outs with —

trouble? — coming up. The Cinderella Kid, still with fire in his eyes. For two innings, same as before, he'd hardly said a word, not even to Olive. But he'd stopped looking like someone had a choke hold around his throat. Just the opposite: he was angry. Everything about him, from the black look beneath his eyebrows to the way he kept flexing his muscles, from the nervous fidgets to the constant stare he trained on Bull, said so — angry.

"Come on, Kid! Swing! You can do it!

"No batter! No batter!"

"Swing! Swing! Swing! Swing!"

"Swing!" squeaked Olive.

"Win or lose, Kid," I said, mostly to myself. I'd called The Kid a coward. I knew after what he'd been through — beaning somebody and almost getting beaned himself — just getting up at bat and playing right field made him more than that, no matter what happened.

Bull gave me a stony stare, enough to make my knees wobble, rocked backward on the mound, kicked high in the air, and let loose.

One pitch, that's all it took. There was the reassuring wiggle of the bat, a blazing fast ball, and CRACK! — like that — the game was over. The Cinderella Kid had done it, hit the longest home run in the history of Indianwood Field, clean over the center field fence, across the little kids' playground, to where it landed with a splash in the middle of the duck pond. Take that, Poisons! We were 6–4 winners — at last.

After that, The Cinderella Kid and the Basement Baseball Club became friends, not close friends, just friends.

He was a year or two older than the rest of us, which meant that once school started in the fall he made friends with kids in his own class. Every now and then he'd go along with us to the Minigolf, where we'd play golf and give Games the business because he was working so hard, or to the Edgewater Township Theater, or to the Aquacenter, but not often. We did play sports together, baseball, football, you name it, in school and out. Word of his picnic-day home run spread like a dry summer fire throughout the town, so that by the time he started school he already had a *big* reputation. More often than not he lived up to it, and more.

I never told anyone, not even AD, about the newspaper article that Olive showed me, or, except for AD, the part about the psychiatrist. I never told anyone about The Kid visiting me in my basement, when he'd asked me questions about my acrophobia, and I never told anyone, not even my parents — not yet at least — about that. I was more careful, that's all. The Kid and I never talked about any of that stuff again either.

I did ask him this, a couple of days after the exhibition: "You gonna play Pony League next summer?"

"You bet," he answered, wiping his hand across his mouth. A cautious smile wrinkled his face, but even so, I could tell that he meant it.

As for Olive, well, that was . . . er . . . different, I guess you'd say. She practiced sports constantly and just kept getting better and better, always a wanted member of our teams. She had a year left of Little League, but I knew (or thought I knew) that the following summer she'd be our Pony League second baseman. I got razzed like you wouldn't believe about her — she did have a weird way of staring at me — but I didn't mind. In fact, if you must know, I sort of liked the razzing. Don't ask me why. There's no telling about those things, no telling at all. I did end up having a lot of chocolate puddings on her front porch. Olive and Socks became good friends, too, and — talk about trouble — they started an all-girls sandlot team of their own.

"More competition," AD said astutely.

"You'll think I'm crazy," I told him one day, "but as good as organized baseball is, playing on the big diamond, hardball, dugouts and all, I think I like our sandlot games better."

He looked up with surprise from his tuna fish and butter sandwich and said, "My sentiments exactly."